VESUVIUS

By Vic LeClair III

First printing

ISBN: 978-0-615-25509-5

Printed in the United States of America

Acknowledgments

Special thanks to Elaine Gehl, Cheryl Kelly, Sara Behling, authors Curtis Brown and Laurel Mills for verifying something I'm good at...grammar mistakes. I am grateful to Traianos Gagos (Assoc. Prof. of Greek and Papyrology) and Terrence Szymanski from the University of Michigan Library for their help on the knowledge of Roman papyri. To Richard Talbert (Author of "The Romans"), Dr. Jean Berger (Prof. of History UWFV) and Steve Rutledge (Asst. Prof. Univ. of Maryland) for their assistance on Roman history. To my wife Joy whose encouragement and understanding keeps me level, when life becomes uneven.

1

The big white house on the corner of Lincoln and Maez was there as long as most people could remember. Tulips were bunched along the front of the home, their varied colors waiting for the morning sun. Inside, the owner and long time occupant struggled to sleep.

Oliver mumbled, "Parosius...Veturia" and woke suddenly, his pajamas soaked with sweat. It was exactly 3:00 in the morning. He sat up and rubbed his eyes, still seeing an image that both frightened and intrigued him. He shook his head trying to bring his dazed mind back to the present.

This had been happening with greater frequency of late. His dreams were vivid. They took him to a place and time that felt familiar though he was quite sure he had never been there.

Oliver Taneschio had taught his students about the relevance of history. He helped them discover how to learn from the past and how it affects them. The majority of his lessons weighed heavily toward ancient Rome. After his wife Tessa had died almost a decade earlier, he continued to teach his history class to the sophomore students at Washington High School. His long instructional career ended two years ago when, at the age of seventy-four, he was politely asked to take a retirement package. Oliver wasn't the negative type and didn't allow his forced loss of employment affect him. Oliver's physique would be considered above average for a man his age. His dark complexion and just slightly noticeable Italian accent kept the widows at his door asking for sugar. All that remained of his once thick hair however, were the gray patches on the sides of his head.

Most of his life, *time* was something that he never seemed to have enough of. Now there was an abundance of it. Oliver thought often of the students he had taught and the many field trips he'd arranged. He enjoyed the treks to all the places he had treasured in his home state of Wisconsin. Back then, time and money did not allow him to travel far. Every now and then, Oliver attempted to convince the school board of the need for a trip to see historic cities. The answer was always the same.

He recalled his grandfather's stories of ancient Italy and wanted his students to feel the same excitement he felt. Oliver himself had been born in Sorrento, Italy, though his father and mother had moved to the States when he was just three years old. Long ago he resigned himself to the possibility that he might never return to Italy, might not ever get the chance to explore the places of his grandfather's stories. Now that he had the time, he could not bear the thought of going on such a trip without his beloved Tessa. Besides, his four children and seven grandchildren needed him. Lately, though, he felt as if someone was pushing him. Like time was running out.

His family did not visit him as much as they used to. Some of them had to travel too far; others were working too many hours. The family still held to a strong Roman Catholic faith and Sundays were happy days for Oliver. At least at church he could visit with some of his kids and grandkids. Still, he intended to be available to them at all times in case they needed help or just wanted to talk. His granddaughter, Cassandra, would be the exception. She was the youngest of his grandchildren. At 23, she lived only blocks away. Every Sunday, after mass, she stopped in to make her grandfather a dinner. Back in 1915, Oliver's parents moved to Crystal River, Wisconsin and much of the family still resided in the town. His home is the same large two-story house that his father built over eighty years ago. Cassandra was the third Taneschio to graduate from the University of Wisconsin - Madison, just ten miles north of her home. She majored in anthropology. As with many graduates during times of economic struggle, Cassandra was unable to find a job in her chosen field. Though archeology was the part of her major she enjoyed the most, her current employment involved fitting suits in the men's department of Trader's Men's Wear, instead of digging up old bones. She resembled her late grandmother, Tessa, in intelligence as well as beauty. For Oliver, Cassandra's long dark hair and milk-chocolate eyes was a constant reminder of years gone by.

Maybe I'll tell Cassandra about the dreams today, Oliver thought while changing his pajamas. *Nah…better to keep it to myself. No need to give anybody reason to believe that an old man's mind might be slipping.* His note pad rested on the nightstand as always and again, as always, he made note of his dream and the continuing story it delivered to his mind. Before returning to bed, Oliver opened bi-fold doors and stared at the dozen pressed shirts that hung neatly on the closet pole. He pushed them to one side, revealing a safe mounted into the wall. Actually, it was more than a safe; it was a small climate controlled container. He bent over and stretched his hand into a ratty, old slipper. Retrieving a key, he opened the safe and removed a golden box. Oliver sat down on his bed and lifted the ten-inch square lid. He removed a letter written in ancient Latin on a papyrus that was pressed between two thin pieces of glass. The papyri was jagged, worn, and pitted, but the letters were surprisingly dark and readable considering its age. It read:

"SEPTEMBER, PER VICIS AB TITUS... EGO DELLEGO NEX...

"September, during the time of Titus... I attribute the death of my daughter not to the destruction of the sea port, but to myself. Veturia was my light when darkness befell. Her devotion and love for her father was limitless until I drove her away with my stubborn traditionalism. I also confess that I was at least partly to blame for the eventual death of a good man, of whom my Veturia loved, Parosius Tacitus.

Had I been the father I should have been her presence in Herculaneum would have been avoided.

Forgive me, my daughter. Perhaps we will meet again."
Veturius Fortunatus

Under the confession was another letter, again lying between two pieces of glass. It was in deplorable condition—scorched as if saved from a fire. The top-half of the letter was dark in some areas, but readable. A burned out area took most of the bottom half, save a few words. Oliver read it in English:

"Dear father,

I am frightened and write in haste...the ground as well as the sky cracks with anger. Was it I that caused the gods to be angry? A daughter needs the love and blessings of her father. Can we not come to an agreement? I cannot live with your disapproving eyes, just as I cannot live without my Parosius. Now your builder holds my heart, and we have made vows to follow our destiny. Do not let blood govern love. Let us be a family that grows strong with your blessing. I miss you, Father...the mountain rumbles...I must...tell Mother I am sorry...the pharaoh's gem rests beneath your chair of honor.

Oliver re-read the sentence in Latin, *"Pharaoh's gemma dormio subter uestri sella veneratio."* Just below that point in the letter, a portion was badly damaged and only a few more words were visible until the rest of the scroll was burned or missing.

The remaining words... *"scrinium...Janus...mucro ...ut Parosius...* were a broken reference to a chest of perhaps a god, a sword and the before mentioned, Parosius. Not enough to make much sense of it. The letters were written in a difficult cursive Latin. Oliver believed that since both letters were from different people and the handwriting looked to be from the same person, they had to have been dictated to that same person. Perhaps, it was written by a well-read slave. He closed the lid to the golden box. He carefully ran his wrinkled fingers over the cover that portrayed a marble image of the goddess Isis holding a golden sistrum. The Egyptian goddess of heaven was a favorite of many ancient priests, and in Rome they held strong to their rituals.

Oliver's grandfather, Demetri, had been a laborer in the excavation of many sites, having worked in Rome, Pompeii, Herculaneum and many other places. Although his formal learning was limited, he eventually became an expert in the field. His hard work in the mid-1890's paid off, and he was eventually promoted to supervisor. Although keeping artifacts was typically forbidden, Demetri Taneschio proudly told his family that such was his reward for his years of loyal and honest work. He was told it was found under an old villa in Rome, not far from the Colosseum. This fact always seemed odd to Oliver since ancient papyri were not typically found in Rome. Herculaneum, Pompeii and Egypt were all places that lend themselves to the conditions needed to keep papyri from decomposing, but this was truly an odd find for Rome. After translating the ancient letters, Demetri spent much of his retirement years trying to find what Veturia may have hid.

Oliver learned that the scrolls were written in AD 79, and that the rumbling mountain was Vesuvius. His grandfather believed 'the chair of honor' to be the marble chairs assigned to senators of the day and situated in the lower sections of the Colosseum, in Rome. During the time the letters were written, the Flavian Amphitheater was months from completion, but the chairs may well have been in place. Emperor Vespasian may have wanted to honor the senators with the chairs as an early gift to keep their favor. Demetri found only fragments of the chairs still remained. The gem that Veturia mentioned remained a mystery during his lifetime. There were many gems, exquisite pieces of jewelry, that changed hands from Egypt to Rome in exchange for peace or for certain favors. What particular pharaoh Veturia wrote of was difficult to say.

In his later years, Demetri became obsessed with finding artifacts. His focus turned toward Herculaneum. He searched the Herculaneum area as if it held the Holy Grail. Oliver's father, who had already started his own family, could not reason with him. He took his family, as well as his mother and moved to America. They say Demetri died on the site, digging to his last day. Oliver believed that if he did indeed die near Herculaneum he must have known when the end was near. He took the time to send the golden box to his young grandchild, Oliver, just before his last day.

"Why did you give this to me, Grandfather? I can do nothing with it," Oliver whispered to himself.

Oliver thought about how fascinated Cassandra had always been with the box. She would often nag him to see it. She would read the letters over and over, hoping to decipher their secrets. During her college years she'd made it a point to minor in the study of Roman life and language in order to better understand the scrolls.

Oliver returned to bed knowing the more sleep he achieved, the more productive he became during the day. He cursed himself for turning into one of those old men who get up before the sun shows itself. He never thought he would be like that. By 6:00 AM, his aching legs told him it was time to start the day. *Cassandra will be here this afternoon, I'd better clean the place up.* He reached for the phone to call her and remind her to bring some garlic bread. He began to dial, but quickly dropped the receiver when realizing that his granddaughter would not be happy to receive a call at such an early hour.

Oliver was not one to complain. He knew loneliness, and the boredom of life without one's life partner was an expected problem. Many men lose their wives and find it hard to cope. All they know is what they've done for decades. They work for fifty years and retire. No need to take up a hobby, because they could travel with their better half to fill their time. When those plans fail, many men don't know what to do with themselves. Oliver, however, was lucky. He loved to read. He always had the comfort of the printed word anytime he felt the slightest bit lonely. By mid-morning he was resting on his bed reading about the very people he had been dreaming about. His shelves were filled with books, some fiction, but mostly ancient history books and biographies. Hours could slip by unnoticed as he walked the Roman roads with Julius Caesar, or fought in the Trojan War with Aeneas. He was deep into a book on first century Romans when the door bell rang, startling Oliver.

He went to the door expecting to see Cassandra with a bag full of groceries. He had already begun to ask her if she had remembered the garlic bread when he noticed she was not alone. There on his porch stood four of his seven grandchildren. Oliver was confused as he suspiciously looked upon their grinning faces. His birthday wasn't until May—a full month away. Cassandra slipped past him, dropped the bag of groceries on the counter and fetched his jacket.

"Come on, Grandpa. Save the food for next week, we're taking you out for lunch," Jason, the oldest, said. Jason was a hulk of a man, but, belying his bricklayer appearance, spent much of his day at his laptop computer, writing software. Oliver never understood how he could navigate a keyboard with such huge fingers.

"To what can I attribute this obvious act of kidnapping?" Oliver asked in his scholarly voice, though he was smiling ear-to-ear.

"Just get in the van! If you do as you're told, no one gets hurt," Cassandra joked.

Arriving at a quiet home-cooking style restaurant, the group and removed their jackets and took a corner booth.

After receiving their drinks, Cassandra pushed a yellow envelope in front of Oliver.

"What's this?" Oliver asked. He opened it and pulled out plane tickets and a pamphlet with a picture of the Colosseum of Rome.

"A couple of years ago we all got together and decided to work on a project together. We put together a list of your past students from high-school records. You wouldn't believe how many of them remember you and told us how fond of you they were. We told them

11

we wanted to fulfill a dream of yours and asked if they would help us. Say you'll go, Grandpa," Cassandra said, tearing just a bit.

Reaching for his ever present light-blue handkerchief, Oliver blotted some tears of his own. "I don't understand. I am grateful for all of this, of course, but how can I go? I've got the garden to tend and...Tessa...."

"It's fourteen days in Italy, Grandpa. Everything's paid for— your meals, tours, transportation—it's all ready for you. You'll see Rome, Naples, Pompeii, and the place you always talk about, Herculaneum. Say you'll go! Jason, Ted, and Amy will take care of your garden. Grandma would have been happy to see you go, I just know it. And we had enough money for two."

"That's right, Grandpa. Cassandra's going with you. It was her idea. She did most of the work. You'll take pictures and write in your journal, and we'll all get together when you get back," Amy said. The tall, thin young lady gave Oliver a hug and nodded her head at her twin brother, Ted. He was the male version of Amy in looks and stature.

"Here's a little something for your trip, Grandpa," Ted said handing him a small statue.

"Ah...Hercules, the protector of long journeys. I thank you, Ted. It seems all of you have done a thorough job planning this adventure. If I were to agree to such a thing, when would we depart?" Oliver asked, starting to get his composure back.

"We deport from Chicago's O'Hare Airport on May 12th, your 75th birthday. You'll have plenty of time to get your things in order. Now do we have an agreement or do we have to get rough?" Cassandra asked with a horrible Edward G. Robinson impersonation.

"Since you put it that way, I believe it's an offer I can't refuse. I'm a little too excited to eat. You best take me home so I can get started on those thank you cards."

"Grandpa, there were over a thousand students who responded."

"Then it's about time I get started. I tend to get a little long winded in my letter writing."

Oliver didn't think his grandchildren fully understood how truly touched he was by what they did. He reached in his back pocket and pulled out a ticket of his own. He didn't want to spoil the unselfish gift his grandchildren had given him and reveal his own plans to go to Italy. A month earlier, call from an old colleague had persuaded him to come to Herculaneum, and Oliver was convinced it was time to make the trip. To stand on the same ground and smell the same air that the Romans did could not be done through his books. He would see about returning the ticket and never mention it to anyone.

The nightly ritual of his intense dreams now seemed to linger during the day. He placed a notebook next to his night table and began to capture much of what went on inside his head. It was as if someone was trying to reach him...as if a story needed to be unraveled.

The weeks went by quickly, but on departure day both Oliver and Cassandra were ready for the early flight. Cassandra stayed the night and got Oliver's Chevy Lumina packed. They made some popcorn and watched the video tape that came from the travel agency. What followed was nonstop discussion and nervous excitement. When they finally felt the need for sleep, Oliver left the room and returned with a carton and handed it to Cassandra.

"What's this?"

"Open it."

Cassandra recognized it right away.

"Ever since your great-great-grandfather gave me this I knew it was meant to be handed down. It is yours now," Oliver said as she opened the box of Isis.

"I can't accept this, Grandpa. What about Jason? He's your oldest grandchild."

"It can only be yours. You're the youngest, as was I. But it's more than that, it's a feeling…like when you know something's right. This is right. I remember when I would occasionally show the box and its contents to my students. I would always end by saying that someday I would go to Rome and find whatever Veturia hid beneath her father's chair. Of course I knew the chair was no longer there, but just the thought of it put dreams into their young minds. I think there is a mystery in the little box that needs to be solved. We just don't know what it is yet."

Oliver walked Cassandra to her father's old bedroom.

"See that cross on the wall?" Oliver asked, not waiting for an answer. That's where your father and his brother knelt and prayed each night before they went to bed. Of course, they were much younger than you are now."

Cassandra stared at the spot.

"Goodnight, grandpa. Sweet dreams!"

"Oh, I'm sure I'll dream. I don't know how sweet they'll be," Oliver whispered to himself as he walked out.

Cassandra looked back at the small area where her father once knelt and did the same. There, she began to silently pray. She talked to God about lost lives, hopeful futures, and the trip she and Oliver were about to embark on. She felt a certain security being where she was and had a powerful sense that her words were being heard. Cassandra then cried, just a little, before standing and going to bed. Tomorrow she told herself she would be strong and leave her comfort zone. It would be the start of an adventure and, who knows, maybe a new life.

Both of them thought they were too wound up to sleep, but by midnight they were in their beds and out like a light. Cassandra woke just three hours later, however. She sat up. Breathing hard, she caught herself screaming and quickly stopped. Oliver didn't hear his granddaughter in the next room. His dazed consciousness was in the same state as Cassandra's. Both put on their slippers and were surprised to see each other enter the kitchen.

"Couldn't sleep either, huh, Grandpa?" Cassandra asked, still reeling from the dream she just woke from.

"A little excited, I guess," Oliver understated.

They both decided to stay up. Two hours later they were on the road. While Cassandra drove, Oliver told Cassandra more about his love for ancient history and how her grandmother, Tessa, would hide his books, because he wasn't spending enough time with her. "The more she hid my history books, the more I confiscated her romance novels. By Christmas that year we had a truce and ended up

15

giving each other a box full of our own books. After the accident, when she couldn't read anymore, I read those silly novels to her."

"You were lucky to have each other, Grandpa. I hope I find someone to share my life with some day."

"You will. What about that *Benny* fellow you were with last week?"

"He's okay, but we have little in common; he's shorter than me, he cries a lot, and he lives with his mother—other than that, he's a perfect match," Cassandra said with a wink.

Cassandra's history with men left much to be desired. Her first real boyfriend, Ross Jouner, lasted nearly three years. The two were together throughout her last two years of high school and the first semester of college. The amount of time spent together didn't always equal the knowledge gained on how best to grow together. A future marriage was happily discussed, but each understood it meant sacrifice. Not the kind of sacrifice that a couple learns from having a child—the kind that eats at what they might be missing. With Ross going to the local tech school and Cassandra attending the state university, distance wasn't a factor. What gnawed at both of them was the lack of what life had to offer. They might never have experienced other love...the passion...the adventure...and the mystery that those bonds tend to clarify. They were held together by the fear of losing the love they had found, and finally, it wasn't enough.

After parting ways, Cassandra dated sporadically but had yet to find the one that would not only replace her first love, but someone who could fill that empty feeling of a passion not yet satisfied. In her mind, this trip would be a welcome diversion from the sad slate of bachelors in Crystal River.

"Speaking of Italy," Oliver said trying to change the subject. "I called an old colleague of mine last week—a Professor Steve Stowald at BYU, where he's involved with conducting spectral imaging on old carbonized Herculaneum scrolls.

"Really, what did he say?"

"Stowald and his lab crew are attempting to decipher what was written on hundreds of papyri that they found. The lab is located right above Herculaneum. The process is very slow and tedious. They continue to do excavating as well. He was happy to hear from me and mentioned that our timing was perfect. They're digging a new site near the Villa of the Papyri, as well as opening a few more boat chambers. They think it might be as exciting as the *beach find* in 1982."

2

Buried just over nineteen centuries, more than one hundred skeletons were discovered and excavated from the ancient beach and boat chambers of Herculaneum—a resort town. It was named after the deified hero Hercules and rests ten miles to the northwest of Pompeii. Overlooking the ruins stands the luminous presence that is Mount Vesuvius. Its devastating eruption in AD 79 left a lasting impression on its surrounding land, as well as the people. At midday on August 24th, Vesuvius erupted violently. A cloud of ash and pumice was sent miles into the air, drifting toward the southeast direction of Pompeii and Stabiae. The next day, the cloud collapsed, and Herculaneum became the victim of a pyroclastic flow. The ground-hugging avalanche of hot ash, pumice, rock fragments, and volcanic gas rushed towards the town at speeds of up to 70 miles per hour.

When Vesuvius was finished, Pompeii was covered in 12 feet of debris. *Herculaneum* was another story. With debris temperatures greater than 500° C, the ash, pumice, and rock fragments flattened and welded together. The town was buried under 65 feet of flow. It was like a giant plaster cast stopping time and preserving the town for all of history.

Until the discovery at the beach, it was believed that the locals left the area in time. Other boat chambers and much of Herculaneum is yet to be uncovered. Also falling victim to Vesuvius was Boscoreale and Oplontis. It is estimated that a total of over 3,360 people died.

Some people are fascinated by the stars, others by new technology. Oliver Taneschio's love was ancient history. When he picked up the morning papers in August of 1982 and read about skeletons discovered on an ancient Herculaneum beach, the tenth-grade teacher knew he had to go see it for himself. With his tickets bought, he and Tessa reached for the door when the phone rang. It was his son Quinn, whose wife Jessie, was in early labor and in trouble.

Oliver and Tessa raced to the hospital and arrived just in time to say goodbye to Jessie. The loss of their daughter-in-law was painful, but could have been much worse had the infant not been saved. Jessie and Quinn's daughter was named Cassandra. It was a horrible, emotional day for the Taneschio family. It wasn't until a week after Jessie's funeral that Oliver reached into his pocket and retrieved the dated airplane tickets to Italy. He decided it was a trip that was never meant to be. Months after Cassandra's graduation from college she lost her father in a fatal car accident on a slippery winter's night. Her bond with her grandfather only grew stronger. Through the years Cassandra continued to hold an unjustified block of guilt on her shoulders. Had she not been born, her mother would still be living. Had she not called her father to pick her up after her car got stuck in the snow, he would not have died. Outwardly she was a cheerful person, but with a heart that, at times, felt heavy. It was her bond with her grandfather that kept her strong...that and their mutual interest in Roman history.

Herculaneum is held in a cement cocoon, preserving a time that was. Papyri, tools, shops, community baths and the people who enjoyed them were stopped in an instant and stored as if something out of a Twilight Zone episode. Oliver could have gone to his grave knowing his dream was not fulfilled. He would have accepted it. But now...now with this last chance, he was not going to let it slip. Sometimes fate, chance, and luck get mixed into each other. This time it was only fate. Oliver and Cassandra were on a trip that felt preordained.

3

Just before boarding their plane they turned around and were surprised to see about fifty family members, as well as some of Oliver's old students. There was just enough time for a few hugs and some handshakes before they were called to take their seats. For Oliver, the send-off couldn't have been better.

The sight of Rome from the sky excited Oliver and Cassandra to no end. They hurried off of their plane to find their luggage. The tour bus was waiting across the street. It seated three travelers on each side. Oliver followed the line of tour passengers and was directed to a window seat. Cassandra took the middle, while a petite woman of Asian descent completed the row.

"I'm Cassandra and this is my grandfather, Oliver. We're from the U.S., ah…Wisconsin," Cassandra said extending her hand. "…and you are?"

"Mee!"

"Yes,…you."

"Mee! My name is Mee Lee," she laughed. "I always start an introduction with Americans that way. Sometimes it runs into a long Abbott and Costello routine. I'm a little tired, otherwise I would have kept it going," she said in perfect English.

Cassandra looked at Oliver who winked back and said, "I think we're going to get along just fine. There's very few of us our age on tour, I hope you're staying for the whole trip."

"I'm never really sure what I'll be doing from one minute to the other. I'm not much for structure," Mee answered.

"Sounds like a fun way to live," Cassandra said, reaching into her carry-on for the golden box of Isis. She opened the box and revealed its contents of scrolls. "I've read these scrolls a hundred times. They hold unanswered questions. Ever since I was little I've been fascinated with Rome and the buried cities. Grandpa's been interested in Herculaneum and Pompeii for a long time. This is our chance to see the real thing, and maybe piece together the meaning of the scrolls."

Staring at the shimmering box, Mee immediately thought back some twelve years. Her brother, Chue, was a high-school sophomore and, as he sat in class, was mesmerized by an object that was being held by a teacher in a history class. He was fascinated to hear the elderly instructor read the words that were written on the old scrolls. Mee and Chue's family moved to California the next year, but her memory of the golden box never faded.

"I'm not much on history. What do you expect to see there?" Mee asked, staring at the contents of the box.

"I guess mostly Roman remains. I suppose they find artifacts for their museum in Naples every now and then, but we would like to learn more about the people and how they lived."

Mee laughed, "I don't like old dead people. Might be kind of fun to see them dig up old trinkets, though."

"It's a slow process, but I'm sure you could hang around with us when we get there," Cassandra offered.

Looking around the bus, Mee said, "It's got to be more fun than hanging around with this old crowd. No offense, Oliver."

"None taken. My granddaughter came along to keep me out of trouble. What brings you to Rome, Mee?" Not waiting for the answer... "I didn't notice you on the plane. Were you on an earlier flight?" Oliver interjected, as he motioned to have Cassandra return the golden box to her bag.

"Lots of questions. Let me guess, you are or were either a cop or a lawyer," Mee ascertained.

"Neither. I was a teacher. Not very interesting..., let's get back to you."

"I was on the flight right before yours. I'm actually from Los Angeles. My folks are from South Korea. I'm here for fun, excitement, and men...like the one that just entered the bus. Oh...and to get away from my family. They were driving me nuts, you know? Isn't he cute?" she said, nodding her head to the front.

"I wouldn't be a good judge on whether the boy is cute or not. What do you think, Cassandra? Is he cute?" Oliver teased.

"Yes, Grandpa, he's cute, in a blond surfboarder-type of way."

"Well then, it's unanimous," Mee said. Let's flip a coin for that empty seat next to him. What do you say, Cassandra...heads or tails?"

"That doesn't seem right...flipping a coin over the right to ...." Cassandra took another look at the handsome stranger. She then reached in her pocket for a small mirror, and adjusted her hair. "Call it in the air, Mee!" she said.

"Tails!" Mee called out.

"Tails it is," Cassandra said dryly.

Mee grabbed the mirror out of Cassandra's hand and looking at herself, said, "I won't be long, just going to get acquainted."

"Take your time. I got all the man I need right here," Cassandra said, hugging Oliver's arm just as the bus started moving.

"You sure were curious about Mee, how come?" Cassandra asked after Mee left her seat.

"After teaching so long you start to know when someone is lying. I don't feel right about her. It's probably nothing."

"She seems pretty nice to me."

"Tell me something, Cassie."

"You haven't called me Cassie since I was a little girl. I think I like it. I'll call you, Oliver. We'll make believe you're my sugar daddy."

"Oh, stop it. I called you Cassie, because what you just did reminded me of the time we were celebrating your seventh birthday. There was a little girl at the party. What was her name? I think it was Jayna…Jayna Burton. She was a bit of a bragger. You hated her with every fiber of your being. Your father said you had to invite her, because she was his boss's daughter. She bit into a piece of your cake and started gasping for air. I saw you stuff something in there before you served it to her. I also knew there was left-over pizza in the refrigerator topped with jalapeno peppers. I didn't say a word then—I didn't like her either. But now I have to ask you…. the coin was heads-up…why did you lie?"

Cassandra sat back and took a deep breath, as if a judge had just read her the guilty verdict. "The next one is going to be *the* one. He didn't strike me that way."

"There's nothing wrong with being picky." Oliver had that certain look on his face that people get when they're up to no good. "I have an idea. Now that we're in Rome, let's do as the Roman's did. Maybe you're just sick of making choices. God knows I wouldn't know which way was up if I had to start dating again."

"I don't think I like the sound of that. What do you have in mind?"

"The 1st century women of Rome would never choose whom they wanted to marry. That was the pater's job...in this case...the grandfather. I have until our last day here to pick your betrothed."

"Okay, I'll play along. It can't be any worse than my past selections. What happens if I don't like your choice?"

"Oh, you cannot reject the man given to you. You must obey. It is said that your virginity is not entirely yours. One-third of it belongs to your father, one-third to your mother, and only one-third to you. The punishment for not agreeing to such a union after I have surrendered a dowry and your rights to your future husband could be death, but more likely a severe beating."

"Okay, now you're starting to scare me," Cassandra joked. "And about that virginity thing...ahh, never mind."

"When the time is right, I'll tell you who the right one will be."

"Then I will make sure to marry him. I'm allergic to severe beatings." She thought for a moment and then reached out her hand and patted her grandfather's arm. "I agree to your proposal with one stipulation. I get to pick a suitor for you. Now wait...not for marriage...just a date. Is it a deal?"

"Oh, I don't think…me? Who'd go out with an old man like me? I wouldn't know what to do. What would I say?" Oliver stammered like a shy teenager.

"Is it a deal or isn't it?"

"Are you saying I'm chicken? Because if that's the case, you've got yourself a deal," Oliver said competitively, solidifying the arrangement with a handshake.

"Good, because I choose her," Cassandra said, pointing towards the back of the bus.

"Already! You've chosen already? This is to be done with painstaking research, interviews, and a touch of gut feeling. To what can you attribute the quality of your pick?" an incredulous and nervous Oliver asked.

"I noticed her on our flight over. I even talked to her for a while when you were sleeping. Her name is Ida. You might as well get it over with. She can sit in Mee's place."

Oliver raised one eyebrow. "I'll do it on my own time. I have two weeks."

Moments later, Mee returned with the biggest of smiles. "He's not only cute to look at, but he has money. We're going out tonight. Sorry, Cassandra, I'm sure you'll find one for yourself."

"Sometimes things happen that you have no control over. I think I'll leave my love life in the hands of a higher power," Cassandra said, looking at her grandfather.

The tour was to be escorted, but Cassandra made sure there would be plenty of free-time for her grandfather to go off on his own.

Oliver was like a small child with his first train set. That first day was a carefree stroll through a portion of Rome with his granddaughter. The Eternal City's abundant sights seemed overwhelming to Oliver. He talked about nearly everything he saw as if he'd lived in Rome. He'd taught, read and re-read ancient Roman history his entire adult life. This was his magical time. He would take in all that he could and not take anything for granted. The tour bus would take them to the ancient ruins later in the week.

On this day, they walked along the Tiber and took their time visiting the Villa Borghese Gardens. The smell of spring flowers was as delightful as that of the fresh bread and tasteful house wine they were served at the Ostaria da Giovanni Ar Galletto. Feeling comfortable in the outdoor seating, Oliver glanced over his menu and noticed Mee Lee and her date across the way. Cassandra sat with her back to their new friends. Contented, she listened to her grandfather reminisce about his younger days, something she'd done so many times before as a little girl.

Oliver put down his menu and stared at his granddaughter. Her resemblance to Tessa took him back to when he'd first met her. "Your grandmother was just a year younger than you are now when we met. I was in my second year of teaching when our principal held a meeting to introduce a new faculty member. I remember being in a bad mood that day. I guess I felt like I should have been more than a high-school teacher by that time in my life. Instead, I was stuck in Crystal River, Wisconsin, trying to feed history to a bunch of sophomores who decided they would never need to know any of what was taught." Oliver rubbed his right temple, as if to massage the memory out of him. "About a dozen of my fellow teachers gathered as Principal Abernathy asked us to welcome Tessa Brull to our school. I was busy feeling sorry for myself and barely looked up from the papers I was correcting. I might not have paid any attention at all if Tessa hadn't stood up and spilled coffee all over the front of her sweater. When no fewer than six of my comrades jumped up to offer her their handkerchief, I figured I'd better have a look. This is the part where you would expect me to tell you that your grandmother was the most beautiful and radiant being that my eyes ever had the pleasure to see, but that would be a lie. Her black hair was up except for unwanted strands that fell and got stuck to her sweaty cheeks. She was wearing thick black glasses, and her skirt was long and looked like it would fit in nicely at the library."

"Grandpa, did you ever tell this story in front of Grandma? It's not exactly flattering."

"Let's just say I left out some of it to protect the innocent—me. Back then, like now, I was a bit thick when it came to women. When my fellow teachers finally sat down I noticed that if you looked beyond the hair, the glasses, and the huge coffee stain, she had a great shape and her nervous smile was quite captivating, *which explained the attention she was getting*. My mind was carrying on just like that of the other teachers, but I didn't show it. I've always been competitive when it involved something important to me. After her first week, I found out three things about your grandmother; she had turned down three prospective dates, she was very attractive when she removed her glasses, and she had two very protective big brothers."

Oliver continued, "A great man once said, 'It's best to neutralize the electric fence before stealing the chickens'. In other words, I needed to get on her brothers' good side. I was able to acquire three Green Bay Packer tickets and invited your great-uncles to join me. The next day I asked your grandmother out to the movies, and she accepted. Her brothers didn't even follow us. That night I had the pleasure of protecting her from the tense moments up on the screen."

"What were you watching?"

"I had the foresight to bring her to Hitchcock's *Rear Window*."

"You devil. Let me guess, the rest is history."

"If you could ask your grandmother how we got together, her version might be a little different. But, yes, I'd say that's about it."

"What about the moral? Don't you always end with a moral?"

"You're older now. No need for a moral. I was just thinking how much she would have enjoyed this trip."

"I miss her too, Grandpa."

The entire day was perfect. Cassandra was just happy to be away from her daily life and spending time with her grandfather. Oliver felt he had arrived in heaven. He was not only in the best place he could imagine, but he took pictures and wrote in his journal to prove he was there. The only thing missing was Tessa, but he would go to the cemetery and tell her all about it as soon as he got back home.

Sleeping in a strange place can be hard, but Oliver had plenty of fresh air that day and fell fast asleep. Around three in the morning Oliver sat up suddenly, sweat pouring from his body. It was the dream...the same people...the same names. This one had an aura of finality. Oliver entered it in his notebook as he had written up the earlier ones. He didn't know why he wrote them down—maybe because they were so real. They haunted him like a song you hear one morning and are still humming the next day. Writing it down was an attempt to let it slip out of his mind.

The next two days were filled with the sights of Florence and more. Although Oliver enjoyed his visit of the city and that of Dante, Boccaccio, Botticelli, and DaVinci, he was eager for his tour of Naples, Herculaneum, and Pompeii. They would go further north to Venice during their fifth day before backtracking and arriving at their hotel in Sorrento on day six. Sorrento overlooks the Bay of Naples, and it is from there they would motor north to the ruins of Herculaneum.

4

Oliver and Cassandra were having the time of their lives, and the anticipation of what was ahead made them eager. The legend of mermaids luring seamen to their death with sweet songs belongs to Sorrento. After taking in the sight of the blue gulf of Naples, Oliver and Cassandra were finally on their way to the ruins of Herculaneum. Much of the ancient city was still buried under Ercolano, its history yet to be discovered.

By early morning the temperature was cool, but slowly warming. The group of about twenty tourists stepped off the bus and was told they could either stay with their tour guide through the wonders of Herculaneum or go off on their own for several hours. They were warned however, that the tour was scheduled to visit Pompeii yet today and they needed to leave on time.

Oliver put his arm around Cassandra and led her away from the tour group. The sun disappeared behind dark clouds as the two walked one mile straight down a hill. They stopped on a bridge as they reached the northeast corner of Herculaneum. Uncharacteristically, Oliver and Cassandra hurried their inspection of many of the ancient houses. They were enamored by the preserved status of the homes and the obvious wealth of some of the larger villas. However, Oliver was to meet his old friend Dr. Stowald in about an hour. A stickler about being on time, Oliver wrote down his notes feverishly as Cassandra took pictures. They crossed such roads as Cardo III, which ran from the ancient coastline inland to the North and the Decumanus Maximus running in an East/West direction parallel to the old coast, when rain began to fall.

While the House of the Mosaic Atrium was all that Oliver had hoped for, he took a special fascination with the House of the Stags. This was a large, stately home named after two statues found in its garden. One was of marble and represented a pack of hounds viscously attacking a deer. The other depicted the deer falling helplessly to its prey. The house was considered quite modern, and evidence showed that it was built after the devastating earthquake of AD 62. A large addition had been built at some point—its use unknown. Passing through the vestibulum, they walked to the side of a marble impluvium, its rain pool still working like a waterfall dropping from the compluvium above. Its effect was soothing and it seemed to bring out a pleasant scent in the air, like the smell of lilies-of- the-valley. Cassandra was comforted by imagining the same sensations as the family who occupied that space in August of AD 79. Oliver, on the other hand, felt a cold sweat pour over him. He stared at the flow of water as if in a trance. A feeling of déja vu preceded a sudden dizziness.

Cassandra caught Oliver before he fell. "Grandpa, are you all right?"

Oliver leaned weakly on his granddaughter. "Just a little light-headed." Scanning the room he added, "I've been here before."

"That's impossible. Maybe you saw some pictures or..."

He gathered himself and stood straight. "You're right. How could I have been here before? Yet, I feel like I know this place as I do my own home." He took out his note pad and slowly sketched several objects. He penciled in one after another, making sure to include the smallest of details. He then ripped the page out, and folded it, putting it in his shirt pocket.

"What was that?"

"Something I've always wanted to do."

Moving through what may have been an office, they reached the peristylium. The garden was, by far, the largest portion of the villa. Unlike most gardens of the wealthy, this one did not have the usual colonnade. Instead, the columns were replaced with windowed walls, each painted skillfully with the playful antics of cupid. As Oliver examined the walls, he heard Cassandra giggling near the far west corner. He followed the laughter and came upon two large statues. The smaller one portrayed a drunken satyr with his flask of wine. The larger one depicted Hercules. The big man appeared even more inebriated and in the midst of urinating against the wall...much to Cassandra's amusement.

"Well, they didn't lack a sense of humor."

"Cover your eyes, Cassandra, give the man some privacy. Have you no shame?" Oliver joked.

"I'm not the only one with zero in the shame department. Who posed for that? If you know, I'd like to meet him."

"I can't help you there. Besides, he might be a tad old for you by now." Oliver retrieved the earlier sketch from his pocket. "Take a look!" he said, handing it to Cassandra. It showed both Hercules and the satyr. The half-man and half-goat figure was drawn in the staggered disposition of the statues themselves. Next to the satyr Oliver drew Hercules, complete with his lack of bathroom manners.

"How did you know that?"

"Haven't you ever had a sense that you've been through something before? I have, plenty of times. I'm not saying I'm a fortune teller, or that I have extrasensory perception, but sometimes things feel extremely familiar to me. I always wanted to write it down and see if it meant anything. This time, I think I saw this place in a dream—a seemingly never ending dream. Coming in here forced me to recall that dream. I think that's why I became lightheaded."

"What else did you draw?" Cassandra asked as she strolled across the back of the garden. They entered a room that butted up against where the villa finally ends. It was completely empty except for a bronze bath tub situated in the middle. This was unusual considering the Roman preference for public bath. The right wall was painted with a beautiful window, portraying the outdoors with the wonders and color of nature. A field of chamomile, violets, and laurel is the background for a wondering purple swamp hen. Drawn out with better than average artistry, Oliver's notepad resembled the room.

"This is incredible. You learned so much about Herculaneum back when you were teaching. Are you sure you never saw pictures of this?"

"Quite sure, remember, I never thought I'd have the opportunity to come here. Besides, had I seen some pictures years ago, I wouldn't have been able to recall the particulars, much less which house they were in."

"What about this cup in your drawing? It looks like the only thing we haven't seen yet."

"I...I don't know. I saw it in my mind. I guess my ESP doesn't work for everything."

The cup referred to was short with double handles. Oliver had scribbled something on its side that looked like tools, and maybe a sword.

Cassandra looked at her watch. "We'd better go, Grandpa. Your professor friend will wonder where we are."

Mee Lee, who was now clinging to her new boyfriend like Velcro, stopped them on the street. "Oliver, Cassandra! We were wondering if it would be okay if we hung around with you for a while. You seem to be the only two in the group who went off on your own. Oh...this is Luke Trettin." Mee poked Cassandra with her elbow. "You know...the one from the bus."

"Nice to meet you. I'm sorry I didn't introduce myself earlier. I guess I'm kind of shy that way." Luke shook their hands strongly and, although he did carry that beachcomber appearance, his voice was strong and articulate.

If Oliver's first impression of Mee had been unsettling, this latest acquaintance proved more so. They both gave him a feel of being phony, as if they were putting on a show. He sensed it would be best to distance themselves. "We actually are meeting some friends...."

Cassandra looked annoyingly at Oliver. "What my grandfather means to say is we'd be happy to have you along. I'm sure Grandfather's friends wouldn't mind a couple of extra visitors."

Cassandra reached for her cell-phone and dialed Professor Stowald. The professor gave them directions to the Herculaneum laboratory. The four walked in a downward angle on a narrow path flanked on both sides by ancient stone walls. They soon found a door on the top of twenty-two steep steps that lead to the ancient beach. Above the door, a sign printed in large blue letters stated, "Funzione Di Ricerca Di Herculaneum."

Doctor Stowald was working in a large room tucked in the back of a moderately sized building. He smiled as they entered his well lit domain.

"It's been a long time, Oliver," the man in a brown lab coat said. Steve Stowald was a short man with weathered skin and snow-white hair. His teeth were big and bright, emphasizing a likeable grin. His walk held a limp that had plagued him since childhood as the result of polio.

"You look good, Stowald—perhaps a little rough around the edges, but all-and-all not bad. I would like to introduce my granddaughter, Cassandra, and our new friends, Mee Lee and Luke Trettin."

"It's a pleasure to meet you," Stowald said to Mee and Luke. Then turning to Cassandra, "So this is the owner of the lovely voice I heard on my phone," the professor said holding out his hand. "I imagine your grandfather has told you how many times I've tried to get him out here to work with me."

"He's told me a lot about you, Professor Stowald, but he never mentioned your kind offers. I can't imagine a more exciting job than unearthing an entire culture."

"Call me Steve. Most people would be extremely bored with my work, and at times it is quite humdrum. For me, it started as an interesting visit and has turned into a twelve-year love affair. Herculaneum has captured my heart and soul and will not let it go. But, please, sit down. I'm sure all of you are tired. I'll get you caught up with what we are doing. After you've rested we'll visit the beach area."

The professor's lab included several scientists and assistants who primarily were removing debris from skeletons on top of tables and recording their findings. The smell of rich earth, mixed with cleaning solution, was everywhere. Pompeii was covered by ash which had hardened around Vesuvius' victims and made it possible to create realistic casts during their final moments. By contrast, the people at Herculaneum were enveloped by hot mud and rock which skeletonized their remains.

While Oliver and Cassandra examined the skeletons on several tables, Mee and Luke wondered over to a heavy glass case that temporarily held dozens of cleaned and recorded artifacts. Earrings, bracelets, various trinkets, gold coins with the head of Nero, and a spiraling golden reptile that once fit the upper arm of a Herculaneum woman sat next to a set of carpentry tools. Luke seemed to marvel at all of it, for the entombment of over 1,900 years had kept much of the Roman possessions like new.

Oliver followed his scholarly friend to a back room filled with white-top table and microscopes. "New technology in imaging has us quite busy, Oliver. As you can see, we have much work to do." The doctor pointed to the multitude of scroll fragments lining the tables. Oliver scanned the room and envisioned the delight he would have in removing the pieces from the glass-topped boxes and deciphering them.

Returning to the front lab, Oliver said, "I think we all feel a need to stretch our legs. Tell me, Stowald, have you uncovered any more boat chambers?"

"Oliver, you've not changed a bit, still direct and to the point. As a matter of fact, we had great success yesterday. We'll visit it soon. Chamber eleven was excavated last month, and twelve is being worked on as we speak. If you wish, we can walk down to the beach now and talk on our way."

Moments later, the five stepped in front of a group of excavators who were carefully digging under the supervision of an Italian Scientist. He was deeply tanned, and his smile was like the high-beams on a fancy car. Cassandra grinned at him, and when he glanced back she felt a bit dizzy. Professor Stowald introduced them to each other. "Cassandra, this is Dr. Sandro Ballantonio.

"You are American?" the handsome young scientist asked.

"That depends. Do you like Americans?" Cassandra asked.

"Some I like, some I don't," the dashing Italian said, putting his hand to his chin. "You, I like."

Cassandra smiled and formed a quick scenario in her mind that centered around this handsome male and several small children playing on the beach next to their summer cottage.

"Would you like to help?" Sandro asked, breaking her fantasy.

"He wants me to help," she said clumsily to Oliver with a giggle.

"I can't let you touch the remains. It's against policy. But you can help remove debris around it."

"Debris is good," she said, unable to remove the smile from her face.

Luke seemed less interested in the current project than in the chamber that had been excavated last month. It was roped off, and two guards held rifles at the entrance. A dimly lit bulb hung from the ceiling deep inside. Under it were various pots and chests resting in a boat, as well as more skeletons.

"Can we see this one?" Luke asked, pointing to the oval shaped entrance.

"I'm afraid not. We haven't found many artifacts in the chambers, but this one was different. A rich Herculanean lady must have had slaves stashing her treasures in the boat. The pots are nice, but the real find is one of the chests. It contains a trove of jewelry, small marble statues of gods, a wonderful soldiers sword, and even some scrolls. We must guard it tightly until we are done with our record keeping and our curators decide on how they want to proceed. Only the Herculaneum Artifact Authorities can enter. If you're interested, I can show you pictures back at the lab," Professor Stowald offered.

"Oh, I doubt we'll have time for that," Oliver interjected. He felt uneasy about Mee and Luke and didn't want Steve giving them any more information than he already had.

"Mr. Taneschio is probably right," Luke said politely and walked back to the other chamber with the rest.

Before entering the site of the current dig, the group was escorted to a boat chamber that had been excavated in 1982. It measured thirty feet deep and twelve feet high. Beyond the dimly lit oval entrance, as many as forty human skeletons and one horse lay hauntingly still. Some specimens remained in the lab for further study, but most had been painstakingly cleaned, dried, and dipped in an acrylic solution to harden so as to preserve them from the elements. They had then been put back in the exact location they were found.

Some skeletons were still in an embraced position. The majority were found lying in strange and sometimes grotesque positions, as if gasping for air. Oliver bent down and looked closely at the three skeletons huddled together. He was not an expert, but he could see that by their length they must have been a man, a woman, and a small child.

Cassandra stood over him. "It's not them, Grandpa. Maybe it's just a feeling, and maybe we'll never find them, but I don't think this is our Parosius and Veturia."

"You're probably right. There doesn't seem to be any jewelry on the woman. A Roman woman of means would have such things. Still, I wonder who they were. What were their names and what were their lives like? Did they come from the sea or were they from Herculaneum?" Oliver stood up and looked at the rest of the human remains. "Stowald, how can you stand not knowing? They all have a story, and we don't know what it is."

"Oliver, we do what we can. Maybe we weren't meant to know their secrets, but I know one thing. They were not cemented in this solid rock tomb to remain that way forever. They were discovered so that we might learn something about them. Romans cremated their dead. As horrible and frightening as it must have been to die this way, they were preserved. Maybe future research will help us with your questions, but for now we go with what we have. Besides, what fun would it be if we had all the answers?"

"Yes, of course—I suppose one gets used to it."

The recent excavation of boat chamber twelve was only just begun. Outside of the entrance, a pleasant but engrossed woman by the name of Sarah worked the beach findings. She wore a white blouse, dark pants, and a look of deep concentration. There, she cleared debris from a skeleton that lay with its skull staring at the chamber—its right arm and fingers stretched out as if reaching for something or someone. The woman explained in perfect English that the skeleton belonged to a six-foot-four man, very tall by Roman standards of the day.

"When we lift him for cleaning we'll know more, but for now I'd say he was a tradesmen of some sort. His size might indicate being a soldier if not for the fact that there isn't any sign of a weapon."

Closer to the sea, the bow of a boat peeked out with pumice partially chipped away. The woman brushed herself off, pocketed a small bone fragment, walked toward the lab without a word.

"Sarah is our bone lady," Dr. Stowald explained. "She's been doing this for a long time. When she has something specific on her mind, everything else seems to get blocked out."

In the chamber, five skeletons were visible. Sandro explained that many more were expected further back in a yet-to-be excavated area. Two of the bodies appeared to be holding back another skeleton near the entrance, which rested on its stomach, facing the remains of the large one outside.

"Sarah measured this one at a little over five feet, probably a young woman," Sandro said.

A large gold bracelet decorated her upper arm. Her fingers pointed desperately out to what was once a beach. It was becoming evident that they were seeing two Roman citizens aching for one another but yet, unable to connect in their final moments.

"We unearthed these two yesterday," Dr. Stowald explained. He could see the sadness in his visitors' eyes as they stared down at the helpless beings struggling in the last second of their lives.

Cassandra looked up at her grandfather with watery eyes. "Veturia," she murmured.

Oliver walked over to the remains of the big one and knelt over it. "Could it be Parosius?" he whispered. As the two skeletons were being freed of the debris that held them for nearly 2,000 years, they were escaping their captivity, but remained very much apart.

Cassandra repeated Veturia's name.

"Cassandra…, what did you say?" asked Dr. Stowald.

"The scroll! Show him, Grandpa. It's them…I know it's them." She scanned the outstretched remains again. "Parosius tried so hard, but he couldn't find her…at least not until it was too late." Cassandra hugged Oliver.

"You may be right, Cassandra. I've had vivid dreams. They played out like three dimensional occurrences imprinted on my mind." Oliver knelt down. "Are you really Parosius Tacitus?" he whispered.

"How could you possibly know their identities, Oliver?" Professor Stowald asked.

Oliver turned away from Stowald and looked deep into his granddaughter's eyes. "We just know."

V

AUC 831 (AD 78) Rome

During the third year of the rule of Nero, Parosius Tacitus was brought into the Roman world.

He grew big and strong following his ancestors in becoming a master builder. He knew his craft, as did his father, Lusius Tacitus. It had been eight years since Lusius had been commissioned to oversee the construction as head architect of the Flavian Amphitheater. His laborers worked under pressure to finish the immense project on time. Located on marshy land between the Esquiline and Caelian Hills, it was to be a spectacular showcase for the Emperor Vespasian to cement his standing with the Senate.

The July air was hot, but the almost complete outside walls made working in the partial shade tolerable. The master builder was stationed in the attic level directing the workers with their erection of Corinthian pilasters as they constructed small square window openings in alternate bays. The entire area was dusty and smelled of human sweat and fresh concrete. Although Parosius had to oversee the entire project, he could generally be found working beside his father, his brother, Cornelius Tacitus, and the many skilled and unskilled laborers. Most of Parosius' crew consisted of slaves, many taken from the Jewish war some years ago. They mixed cement and poured it into large molds. When hardened, they used horses and ropes to drag the heavy wall pieces to their destination. The work was brutal and constant, with supervisors standing over them like lion-tamers.

Lusius Tacitus was the father of six. Only two of his children lived beyond the age of eight. His wife died shortly after the birth of the youngest, Cornelius. Both Parosius and Cornelius were tall and strong, towering over their hard working, balding father. Parosius was known not only as intelligent in matters of building, but as proficient with weaponry—having briefly served during war campaigns. He had handsome features and blond hair. His strong hands and sensibilities were tailor made for his profession. At twenty-eight he was still unmarried. Most men respected Parosius, perhaps because of the confidence that resonated from his personality.

Cornelius was four years his junior. While his brother was given a limited education, Cornelius had the advantage there. His learning was marginal compared to those in the wealthy patrician class, but he *was* able to read and write with exceptional talent. Cornelius was recently married, but by his own admission, he still had a large appetite for women. He had a tendency to live with risk, but always kept his dream of a richer life. What he wanted most was to one day break away from his family history of builder's and make a mark for himself. His quick temper, sharp mouth, and occasional laps of judgment would, on occasion, get him and his family in trouble with those who had the power to do them harm. His marriage to a general's daughter could be both a catalyst for his future endeavors or a curse, depending on his own liabilities. Parosius could be counted on to do what he could to keep Cornelius from going astray, but sometimes even *his* patience would run thin.

Though life was hard for all of the plebian class, they were citizens of the Roman Empire and felt proud as such. The plebs represented ninety-seven percent of the Roman population. They were the working poor—the builders, the shopkeepers, the soldiers, and the blacksmiths. The yearly earnings of master builders were 350 denarii's—more than a common soldier was paid, but they worked hard and earned every bit of their pay. Lusius' once proud quaestorian family was torn down by the powerful, but paranoid Emperor Nero. They had struggled to regain status ever since.

Following a bloody civil war, Titus Flavius Vespasianus became Caesar Vespasianus Augustus upon being proclaimed Emperor in AUC 822. Vespasian was known throughout Rome as the people's ruler. He was stout and had piercing blue eyes. Though not a tall man, he possessed a strong build for a man of his years. His face was tanned and rugged. It held a mouth that curved up in a smirk, as if telling all of those near him that he knew what they were thinking. His eldest son, Titus, was currently tending to foreign affair matters. Titus was a younger version of his father in appearance, intelligence, and fairness—although a bit more ruthless. He was revered by much of Rome for his leadership in the capture of Jerusalem.

Vespasian's father had been a tax collector, and his mother the sister of a senator. Through military savvy and celebrated victories, he became emperor. The great leader devoted much of his time in repairing the destruction the war had caused and restoring discipline in an army that previous Emperor, Vitellius, had allowed to deteriorate. One of Vespasian's first orders of business was putting Lusius and his young son Parosius in charge of the building of a great amphitheater. The emperor wasn't long on detail, but had a vision of what he wanted.

"The people's amphitheater is to be a vast set of tiers holding enough seating for 50,000 spectators. It is to be built around a central elliptical arena. Below the arena, you will build devices that will raise our beasts from their cages below. Spectators will come from all countries to witness such a sight. We will put on shows that will be remembered and written about for all of time." He put his hands upon Lusius, while Parosius stood beside him. "I have selected a committee of senators to work with you on the plans. If they become quarrelsome and divided in their ideas, do not hesitate to see me about it. You and your sons will make trips to Pompeii. You will note what was done well with their amphitheater and improve upon it," and, in a tone that was more of a command than a question, he added, "I trust you agree with this plan?"

"We will not fail you, Emperor. It will be an honor to be a part of such an undertaking," Lusius answered with a bow of his head, and one knee pressing the floor. Parosius would always remember the scent of Vespasian. It was not perfumed like many in such a god-like stature, but of one that toiled in hard work. Despite Caesar's power to end a life with the nod of his head, it wasn't unpleasant to be near him, but comforting, like the smell of baked bread.

"Raise your heads, Lusius...Parosius. How can I tell if you mean what you say if I can't look you in the eye!" the burly Vespasian ordered with a smirk.

That meeting took place in March of AUC 823 and now, over eight years later, the Tacitus family was but a couple of years from finishing the grandest amphitheater ever built. As Lusius' health began to decline, Parosius took over complete management of the build. Parosius, Cornelius, and their father moved from the cramped and noisy second floor apartment they grew up in, to the rent-free back room of Roman senator and lawyer Marcus Voltacilius Pilutus. During the planning they became great friends, although Cornelius wasn't sure if it was true friendship. Pilutus was able to influence certain designs by being close to the builders. Parosius often wondered, *if the project was finished—would Pilutus be the generous landlord that he portrays at this time?*

On this exceedingly long, hot day, Parosius wanted nothing more than to visit the public baths and begin again tomorrow. He was uncharacteristically happy to see an approaching soldier—anything to break things up.

"Parosius Tacitus, the emperor wishes to talk with you. Come now!" the soldier insisted. His expression was straight-forward and non-flinching.

Parosius stood and brushed the day's work off of his grimy garment.

"I won't be long," was all he said as he left.

His father and brother looked concerned and worried about Parosius, while having a few fears of their own. A meeting with an emperor, even with one that they admired, could be very good or very bad. Anyone could have a bad day—but when you were ordered to stand before one of infinite power—anything could happen.

"What did you do?" Lusius asked his youngest son as he measured a distance for brackets that were to hold a velarium for spectator shade.

"I've done nothing. At least nothing that was seen. Do you think the emperor is displeased with our work?"

"We are still on schedule, my son. Perhaps he wishes to make yet another change."

"When I am consul, we will see who makes changes," Cornelius said, surprising his father with a serious tone.

"When you become consul, surely the lions will sprout wings," Lusius joked. As far fetched as his sons comment was he wondered if it was possible. After all, Cornelius was smart, even brilliant at times. His good looks tended to get him into trouble, but with maturity it could help him. He recently was allowed to see a senator's daughter. If taken under the wing of the senator, perhaps, in time, something may come of him.

Parosius followed the soldier past the basilica and down the length of the forum to a municipal building that engineers used for architectural planning. Emperor Vespasian was looking over an oval table, on top of which plans were written on papyri. Three or four senators stood around the table.

"Parosius Tacitus," the soldier announced with his right arm stretched out in allegiance.

"That will be all for now," the emperor said waving the soldier away. "Parosius, I trust all is well with our project."

"Lack of travertine and tufa continue to disrupt, but we are still ahead of schedule," Parosius said with head slightly bowed.

"That is good, Parosius. The need for such supplies has not fallen on deaf ears," Vespasian said as he signaled one of a few senators in the room to come forward. "I want to introduce a good friend of mine, Veturius Fortunatus. Veturius has generously offered to fund an arch in honor of my son, Titus, for his victory in Jerusalem. I, in turn, have agreed to loan out your building expertise."

"In what capacity, Caesar?"

"I wish to build a villa in Herculaneum," the man with the weathered face and noble ancestry interjected. Despite the informal conference, Veturius Fortunatus wore his senatorial toga with the purple border. He was of average build, but had a commanding voice. The highly lit room had shown well his light green eyes and white hair that seemed to glow.

Parosius observed the man, and then looked at the plans stretched out on the table. It was a large retreat to be set in a beautiful resort town overlooking the Bay of Neapolis.

"This is a grand undertaking, over fifty rooms! But if I may be so bold, not like that of the amphitheater. What of my work here…in Rome? What of supplies? Herculaneum is a few days' travel. How will I manage both?" Parosius implored.

Reaching to put his formidable arm around the much taller Parosius, the Emperor said, "Much of what you ask has already been dealt with. Supplies were sent ahead to Herculaneum by boat and await you. More supplies and the laborers can be purchased at Neapolis. Your father and brother will watch matters here during your absence. I will have a coach retrieve you when you are ready."

"And of this crew…are they skilled?"

"If not, I'm sure you'll see that they learn quickly."

"Parosius, I asked for you because I want my villa to be built by the best. I expect you to come to me with any obstacle that may prevent you from doing your job," Veturius said. The senator was a past general of the Roman Army and now a wealthy businessman owning a large measure of land.

So it was decided. These types of arrangements did not involve the Emperor asking the builder for his permission or assessment. Parosius had a service that was needed and he was not only to accept it, but accept it with the honor and respect of his Emperor and that of Rome. Parosius believed in the ways of Rome. Being a Roman citizen meant a great deal to him. He would follow his orders and do his job. At this time in his life he had no ambition to change the way things were. Sometimes things changed on their own.

As a token of the Emperor Vespasian's gratitude, however, gifts were not out of the ordinary. Vespasian ordered a blacksmith to manufacture a special silver wine cup. He was to watch Parosius and make note of him without his knowledge. The engraving was to be precise in its presentation. The cup was incrusted with two monumental Roman buildings of the past. On each of the two handles the blacksmith imprinted a small hammer and chisel. In the center of the cup was the image of Parosius, with his name below. He stood tall, wearing a workers toga and holding the sword given to him by his father in one hand, a hammer in the other. Most knew the sword was special to him. If the emperor knew of its origin, he would have it destroyed and Parosius punished. That secret was between the three Tacitus men, and it was meant to remain that way. His new cup soon became a steady companion to his sword.

VI

The next morning Parosius set out for Herculaneum. He brought with him his trusted life-long friend, Publius Pulcher, a small man with much more brain than brawn. He had a ready smile, a quick wit, and a political tongue. The latter attribute—or affliction—would occasionally cause him, as well as anybody he was with, discomfort. His lifetime argument circled around the brutality brought to slavery. Growing up, Publius had been witness to countless floggings, rapes, and humiliations. Many of the punishments were dealt out on the whims and sadism of their masters and not for crimes committed. One Roman equestrian found that lamprey eels offered him an opportunity to display his cruelty. Those slaves sentenced to death would be tossed into a pond of eels. In such a setting he could better see the sight of a man being torn to pieces. At the same time, many slave owners would force their slaves to service their sexual needs. A jealous wife might very well have a slave severely punished for attracting her husband. Publius made it his business to cure this wrong where he could. Parosius, ever the protector, reasoned that it was a plight much greater than what a single man could change. Publius was more than a friend to Parosius; he could be counted on to keep a sharp and accurate account of expenditures during their project while also lending a hand with manual work.

As they made their way south, the quite visible 6,000 foot Mount Vesuvius concealed its past penchant for destructive behavior. It had been over a thousand years since its last eruption. To the people who resided below, the mountain had been quiet and they saw no reason to fear it. Vesuvius wore green pastures with orchards and vineyards, like a mask. Near the summit was a forest of trees with lively game. The horses were working hard as Parosius and Publius had them hauling a heavy load of building material and enough personal effects to make their stay as comfortable as possible.

"I would hope we would make quick work of this villa, Parosius. The snobbery of the rich makes my skin crawl," Publius remarked.

Parosius looked down at his friend in all seriousness. "I intend to make the villa of Veturius Fortunatus one of envy to all who visit. Not one dimension will be miscalculated. I would advise you, my friend, do not make an enemy of the wealthy that line the Bay of Herculaneum. I'm to be paid a ridiculously high bonus for my services, and I intend to earn it."

"You insult me. When have you known me to cause a rift?"

"More times than I can count, my friend," Parosius said, shaking his head.

"What do you know of this Veturius Fortunatus? Is he the type to treat us as slaves? Will he run out of money and leave the project half done?"

"Surely you've heard of him. Do you live under a rock? He is worth thrice more than Pliny, is well read and owns farms near Pompeii, as well as a fishing business in Herculaneum. His businesses in Rome alone make him one of the richest in the senate."

"Tell me, Parosius, am I too old to be adopted?" begged Publius.

Parosius and Publius angled their load toward the line of mansions that stood proudly above the Bay of Neapolis, as only pedestrian traffic was allowed on the town streets. Upon locating the land allotted to Veturius, the builders stood in awe, taking in the sea breeze and picturesque scenery.

"Only a god should be allowed to vacation in such a place," Publius announced.

"Then let's bed under the stars tonight and be like gods. In the morning you will venture back north to Neapolis. Our workers and supplies await," Parosius said.

"Are you not accompanying me tomorrow?"

"I'll stay behind and place the villa markers. You'll be expected back with enough daylight to begin the foundation work," Parosius ordered while setting down some bedding.

"You bore me, Parosius. I say we mingle among the locals. I hear the taverns along the Decumanus Maximus become lively in the late hours." Publius teased about an unlikely romp to Main Street.

"Already you intend on being a thorn in my side. Tomorrow will be long and hard. We've no room for frivolous entertainment."

"You only need to command and I will follow, my master," Publius said bowing sarcastically.

The sky was full of stars that night. The half-moon created a nightlight for the two from Rome. With the fragrance of wild flowers and tall grass they set down for the night.

Moments later, Publius could hear the even flow of his good friend's breath. Slipping on his leather street shoes, he made his way to town. Herculaneum was not at all like Pompeii. Publius had been to

Pompeii several times before, usually for pleasure. The town was lively and you couldn't walk a block without noticing another tavern. On one such visit, Publius and a group of friends counted over one hundred drinking establishments. Nearly all the taverns employed barmaids whose second career was that of prostitute. Since it was unacceptable for regular women to frequent such places, the barmaids were very welcome sights to the wine-guzzling patrons.

The roads of Herculaneum were clean and relatively quiet. The darkness was slightly interrupted by dim oil lamps that rested on the outside walls of merchants and taverns. After finding a barber who was willing to shave him at such an hour, Publius walked out of the shop and noticed the signs of three taverns down the road. He picked up a stick and threw it to the sky. Wherever the stick pointed was going to be his destination for the night. On the stone wall above the door a mural was drawn of a large drinking horn with grapes bulging out of the top and drips of wine dropping out of the bottom. Above, it read "The Taverna Caepionia." Entering, Publius half-expected to see a higher form of entertainment, after all, this was the town of the rich. Instead, the establishment wasn't much different than those of nearby Pompeii. Written on a far wall was, "Warm wine, and warm sex we will give—for what else is needed for you to live?"

The establishment was a large two story building covering an entire corner of a block. You could enter and leave from either road. Several tall tables were set up for the drinking of many different varieties of wine. At one, several men were playing a game of *knucklebones*. Publius hadn't played the game since he was a child. The dried ankle bones from sheep had four different sides—each with a its own value. Asking what the stakes were, he discovered there was indeed a difference between this tavern and those of Pompeii.

Beyond the bar room was a more tranquil garden area. A barmaid followed him and took his order. She was a large woman; her hair dyed a rich red color. She wore a dark toga. Her face was pretty and not as chubby as the rest of her. When she smiled, Publius noticed a set of teeth that were not at all stained and appeared healthy, but a few were missing in the most prominent areas.

"Wine, s-s-sir?" she asked with a whistle.

"Yes, and you may keep my cup full until I tell you to stop."

Switching from barmaid to whore, she leaned her abundant cleavage toward Publius. "Can I interes-s-st you in anything els-s-se?"

"Madame, I expect that if your ability to pour wine is as good as your skills with a man, we will be doing business through the night. Can I have your name?"

She covered her mouth as if embarrassed and said, "C-c-cec-c-celia."

The gods surely have a great sense of humor, Publius thought while holding back his laughter. "Well, Cecelia, could you bring me some warm Falernian? I know it's made not far from here. It's been a while since I've wetted my pallet with the finer wines."

"I can indeed s-s-sir. I'm afraid it's-s-s not cheap."

"And neither are you I'm guessing."

Cecelia giggled and ran out of the garden. The night ran on with drink, a visit in the back room with Cecelia, more drink, a little gaming, followed by more Cecelia. Suddenly, jolted by a loud snore, Publius thought he had awakened himself. Realizing the noise was coming from his night's partner, who was resting comfortably on the couch next to him, he sat up quickly. His head pounded severely, but that did not stop him from quickly slipping on his loin cloth and tunic. He dropped the few coins he had inside the big woman's shoe and left without waking her.

Publius returned to the campsite just as the sun rose. Parosius was shivering and mumbling in his sleep. Publius thought of his mother having warned him not to wake sleeping dogs. Parosius could be worse than any dog. Using precautions, he found a long stick and poked his old friend. Parosius woke suddenly, snatched the offending stick away from Publius, and stood in defense.

"Why wake me in such a manner? Do you not favor life?" Parosius asked angrily.

"You were dreaming…, loudly."

"Ah, yes, I remember—I was running. The ground was shaking and the skies grew dark. I didn't like the feeling. What do you think it meant, Publius?"

"Homer said, 'A dream comes from Zeus'. You must have made Zeus very mad. But through the dream, I think he has punished you enough. Let it be done."

"You're probably right. A new day is here and with it a bright sun. Let us begin the build."

Publius yawned and wanted nothing more than to see the inside of his blanket. Parosius looked at him suspiciously.

"You didn't!"

"I did and it was great, except for this ache in my head."

"I thought I told you to behave yourself." Parosius reached for Publius and turned his face to the side. "Your cheek is red. Did you cause trouble?"

"I participated in a little game of *knucklebones*. The stakes were high and so was I. I didn't want to play, but Cecelia thought I would win."

"How much do you owe...and who is Cecelia?"

Feeling his swollen profile Publius said, "Let's just say I paid my dues. As far as Cecelia, she is a mountain of a woman...ahh, but what a woman."

The sympathy that Parosius felt for the hangover his friend suffered was nonexistent. He sent Publius on his way and began planning.

Parosius marched off the boundaries of the large villa, measuring the three-hundred foot length by the one-hundred foot width. Each room was meticulously marked. He interrupted his work only occasionally to day-dream about his future. Would he ever be blessed with a family and the riches to build his own home? He could never hope to own one as grand as this. A small, sturdy home would be enough for him.

The day was long and Parosius was glad that no one stopped to annoy him while he concentrated on his work. As the sun began to drop, Parosius could see the large dust cloud of a wagon coming from the north. With the visitors drawing near, he adjusted his view and could make out Publius leading a group of about twenty to his build site.

The spent face of Publius was obvious to Parosius as he dropped from his horse. The wagon of slaves was followed by a man on a horse who proudly wore a freedman's cap. The oval cap signified the slave was now a freedman. It also insured that his sons and daughters would be born free.

"Parosius…meet our foreman, Giton."

The man who went by the single name of Giton was of medium build, but strong where builders needed to be. His shoulders were broad and his legs thick. Like Publius, his facial demeanor was sad and withdrawn. Parosius understood why his friend and new foreman would not look him in the eye as soon as the other men stood before him.

Parosius looked dolefully at the twenty scrawny men with sullen expressions and skin that hung loose on their bodies in purple shreds.

Publius, angry more about the treatment of the slaves than the Emperor's promise of a good working crew said, "Except for Giton, they all worked the mines. None of them knew how long they were subjected to the whims of their overseer, only that they were introduced to the whip daily. We were given those who would not have made it through the week. Although they know nothing of building, I felt I needed to take them."

The summer sun would be blistering, and occasionally tempers would flare. His mind fighting two battles, Parosius tried to make sense out of his agreement to build a spectacular villa versus the sorry tools he was given to achieve his goal. He did not like being in charge of the discipline, but understood he needed to administer consequences when his orders were not followed. Pausing for a moment and nodding his head slightly, he planted his foot on a stout boulder and raised a single eyebrow. Publius knew his friend like no other. As young Romans, that look usually caused their childhood friends to react in one of two ways; listen attentively, or run for the hills. Today it meant he had come to a decision and no one was going to change his mind.

The slaves held their heads down, a few could barely stand. Parosius scanned the wretched beings before him. The togas they wore were threadbare and most were barefoot. "I will provide you with new workman's clothes and cloaks when the cold weather begins. You will be given sturdy wooden shoes. You will not want for food and water."

The slaves slowly lifted their heads and looked at the big man in disbelief. "You will be rewarded for good work. You have been given a chance to have a life worth living. Only a fool would not take this chance and make the most of it." Parosius removed his foot from the rock and stood upright. "Those of you who cause me and my crew the slightest hindrance will be sent back to the mines. You are men and will be treated as such. Tonight we eat and rest. Tomorrow your education begins."

Readying themselves for the night, Publius and Parosius set down near their smoldering fire while the well-fed crew slept. "You're doing the right thing Parosius. Treat them right and they will return the favor. By the way, where are you going to get the money to feed and clothe them as you promised?"

"You are the accountant—didn't you say the material costs have gone up considerably?"

"No. I…oh, right…at least twenty percent. We may have to get word to Veturius to increase our allotment."

"Make the adjustments in the book. I'm afraid the truth of the matter would not go over well. If we complain to the emperor of the workers we received, he will have them killed, or worse, sent back to the mines. He would then send us a new crew. If we ask Veturius for an increase in costs for the slaves, they will likely receive the same fate. Besides, assembling a new crew would take as much time as training this bunch."

"You are undoubtedly correct, Parosius. I will make the changes."

Listening closely to the conversation, Giton looked up as he lay some distance away with his men. Giton was the type to be interested in all that went on around him. His inquisitive nature was what had awarded him his freedom, but from that grew the hatred of those he spied on. Since this ability worked well for him before, he felt no reason to change with his new group of acquaintances.

While in Neapolis, Publius found Giton by setting up wanted signs for the position of building foreman. Any citizens with building experience were to gather at the forum within the hour. Giton no longer felt safe working for the man that made him a freedman. He was known as the household snitch and sleeping with one eye open became a habit. When he approached Publius for the job, he didn't lie about his experience as a building foreman—nor did he come forward with his reasons for wanting to leave Neapolis.

As the weeks went by, the group grew close and many friendships were formed. The slaves began to heal, both physically and mentally. Giton kept close tabs on his men and trained them, as did Parosius. Their training styles differed; Giton's was based on belittling and insults. Parosius allowed them to fail and then showed them how to make things right. Although Parosius found Giton to be a suitable foreman, his continual complaints of certain slaves seemed trivial at best.

By the third week Giton became frustrated with the lack of leeway he was given to deal out punishments. Taking matters into his own hands, he watched as a slave he found particularly offensive paused from breaking up some rock to be removed for an extension of the heavy foundation. Believing the slave to be lazy, he took the whip to him. The slave, Rufus from Capua, screamed from the sudden skin tearing slash. The other slaves watched in silent horror, afraid that they might receive the same. Parosius, hearing the wail, ran to the slave.

"Giton, what has this man done?" Parosius asked while Publius covered the bloodied man with cloths.

"He would rest at a whim. I had no choice. You wouldn't have me discipline them, but it has become necessary."

"Rufus, what did you do to receive such a strapping?"

Rufus looked at Giton and then again at Parosius before bowing his head.

"It is fine. You may speak without retribution."

"I've been working all day. I only needed a moment to rest and sip the water."

"He lies. Who would you believe, me or the ignorant slave?"

Parosius stood between the two men. "You leave me no choice. You will leave this place, Giton. Publius, bring him to the tent and complete his wages."

"You don't understand. He's a slave and must be treated as one. They're not your friends. They would push a sword through your heart if they had a chance."

"Go, Giton. You are through here."

Giton walked angrily behind Publius. Inside the tent, murmurs turned to shouts. Both men were about the same size, but it was Giton who was seen falling backwards out of the tent opening and dropping to the ground. His nose was bleeding profusely.

"You will pay for this. I will make it my business to make sure I get my revenge. You'll see...." Giton shouted as he rode his horse north.

From then on the crew worked well together—aside from a few skirmishes and disagreements along the way. The slave, Rufus, became the new foreman. During the fall season of AUC 831, the villa of Veturius Fortunatus was beginning to take shape. The atrium bestowed a wonderful impluvium. The marble pool collected its rainwater from quadrangular openings above. The beauty of color and grace would not be matched by any other Herculaneum villa. A rich green border circled the marble pool. Four beautiful marble satyrs, each posing in their own form of delight, gazed upon the clean water. The walls held exquisite bronze oil lamps for night viewing. Parosius continued to hold the plan specifications to impeccable accuracy while adding his own ingenious ideas along the way. The winter dining rooms and baths faced west, allowing the sun to warm them in the evening. The bedrooms and reading rooms faced the east for the morning light.

As winter drew nearer, Parosius and a number of his crew worked to develop the peristyle, hoping to finish before the cool weather arrived. This large courtyard was surrounded by the unfinished colonnade. They were raising the pre-built columns when all labor was temporarily halted by a welcome diversion.

She entered through the back garden area. The sea wind carried the scent of her perfume, perhaps spikenard. It was an obvious message that someone other than sweaty men was present. She wore a colorful garment that hung loosely around her neck. A fine gold belt fit comfortably around her slim waist. Her long dark hair lay nicely down her back, but was a bit ruffled from the journey. She was slender, with just enough flesh in all the right places. Beneath her painted face was the look of a pretty but shy young woman. It was obvious to Parosius, Publius, and the rest, that this was someone of worth and undoubtedly from the patrician order.

"I am Publius. How can I be of service?" he said, greeting the lady but careful not to touch her with his dirty hands.

"I am Veturia Fortunatus, daughter of Veturius Agrippa Fortunatus. My mother rests in town. She has business with a physician. I come on behalf of my father to keep watch on his investment," she said with a quick glance at the men, stopping at the sight of Parosius and quickly looking away. "Would the man called Parosius Tacitus be present? I wish to speak with him."

Parosius stood and introduced himself to the smiling Veturia. His first impression of her was of a spoiled rich girl. His crew slowly got back to their building chores. Publius thought about discussing how better off the beautiful daughter of a senate member would be in his capable hands as compared to Parosius, but wisely continued checking over his figures on the papyri.

Veturius Fortunatus' daughter, Veturia, was seventeen years of age. At fifteen she had been meant to wed one Arrius Antonius. This would have been a shrewd alliance for Veturia's father. Arrius was the natural son of a wealthy land owner who carried the blood of the upper-most patrician class. Arrius had his eye on the office of Tribune. This honor would have given him the ability to veto any law that could harm the common people. Arrius was still young however, and needed to prove his worth. His father, who held a symbolic position in the Roman army, held control over Arrius' future. Except for an occasional skirmish, Rome was at peace. In August of AUC 829, Arrius was sent to the Isle of Mona to squelch a disturbance and was consequently killed. When the news of his death reached Rome, the family members of Fortunatus showed opposite reactions. The head of the household and his young son, Crescentius, were distraught and saddened, but Veturia and her mother, Livia Agrippa, were relieved. Their dislike for Arrius held no bounds. They found him arrogant and with the looks of a mule. The young Veturia vowed that her future husband would be a true and trusted man of her choosing. She felt that fate had stepped in to save her from a marriage even the gods would have disapproved.

Veturia was forced to grieve for a time that in her estimation was exceedingly too long. Finally able to dispose of her dark clothing and feeling a need to get away, she begged her father to allow her to visit the site of their new villa in Herculaneum. Veturius granted her request on conditions; her mother would travel with her daughter, and neither was to leave the sight of their escorts. They were also not to change any of his building plans without written permission from him or unless Parosius thought it a reasonable request. Veturia justified the breaking of all such stipulations by reason of convenient forgetfulness. The authority for making changes was not normally given to one with the social status of Parosius, but over the months Veturius had grown quite fond of Parosius' work.

Parosius was not well versed in the ways of women. He was handsome and aware of the attention he received from the opposite sex, but had precious little time to bother with a long-term relationship. An occasional night out with his brother, Cornelius, and friend, Publius, would generally end in a drunken visit to a brothel. That was the extent of his love life. Through friends and family, Parosius had seen the hardships of uniting with a wife only to lose her to an ailment or to child-birth. He did not wish to hurry down that path. Yet, lately he wondered what it might be like to have someone to trust, care for his needs and be at his side at night.

Parosius led Veturia to a room that, upon completion, was to be a library for her father's business. A center table held a set of scrolls on which the villa's plans and instructions were laid out.

"My father holds you in great regard, Parosius Tacitus," Veturia said shyly averting her eyes.

"As I do him. He didn't mention a daughter. What promise did you make to your father to be given permission to travel such a distance without his company?" Parosius inquired.

"I do not need my father's permission. I do as I please…when I please," Veturia lied.

"Very well then, I will be sure to compliment your father on his ability to produce such an independent daughter," Parosius said, amused.

"No need to trouble yourself," she said nervously.

"No trouble at all. I'm sure he would be happy to hear of your liberal spirit."

Veturia looked at him closely. "Are you playing with me, Parosius Tacitus?"

"Never…I am only here to serve," Parosius said, bowing with a touch of sarcasm.

Veturia, by now quite taken with the handsome builder, was beginning to forget why she had come. "Yes, well, thank you. I should be going now. My mother waits for my return."

"Do you not want to examine your father's prints?"

"Oh, yes, of course…the prints. We are here for a few days…perhaps tomorrow?"

"Tomorrow would be good. Will you be bringing your mother?"

"Not if I can…, that is…if she is up to it," Veturia stammered as she backed out of the room clumsily.

VII

In the months to follow Veturia made frequent visits to Herculaneum with her entourage of slaves and was occasionally escorted by her brother Crescentius, who was eight years her junior. The young boy was tall for his age, but painfully thin. His hair was curly and golden brown. He was a quick learner and had that certain aura about him that portrayed a bright future. Crescentius did not hold to snobbery as many in his position might. Like his sister, he was enthralled with the builder, Parosius, and followed his every move. Veturia sometimes wondered if she would ever find Parosius alone. As for Parosius, he found the boy slightly annoying, but clever and quick at picking things up.

Veturia was beginning to cherish her father's villa, but more so its builder. She didn't miss the bustling noise of Rome. Nearly all the workers were gone. With the villa nearing completion, all that remained were a few painters, mosaic artists, Parosius and Publius. The rest were sent to Rome to help with the amphitheater. Veturia took long walks through the hilly surroundings and soon was not only mesmerized by the green colors interspersed with violets and chamomile, but she was captivated when in the presence of Parosius.

On a fall day, as she sat on a blanket overlooking the beautiful Bay of Neapolis, Parosius sat on his horse directly in the sun's path. A cool breeze blew Veturia's hair as she strained to see who approached.

"I'll be finished soon. Your father and mother will be coming for the blessing in a month," Parosius said, not wanting his time with Veturia to end.

The two young Romans talked, brushed up against each other, stared endlessly at each other when the other wasn't looking, but neither took the first step toward embrace.

"Did I not tell you of the latest changes? There are to be many, many changes…and additions too. I expect that it will take weeks to get everything in. Come, sit so I can discuss them with you," Veturia said, smiling devilishly.

"I should get back to work," Parosius said.

"You work too hard." She took his hand and attempted to pull him from his horse. "Today the town's people celebrate *Compitalia.* Let's make a day of it. I've been invited to dinner tonight. My new friends asked that I bring a guest. You wouldn't want to disappoint the town Lares," she said, referring to the ghosts of the sons of Hermes and Lara who protected Roman homes, family, sea and land. "Will you attend with me?" Veturia asked.

"Your friends in town are of …I am only a builder…are you sure?"

"You are a Roman. You will be treated as any guest would be treated. Now, if you won't come down you'll need to pull me up," she said stretching her arm.

"Of course," Parosius said. He reached for Veturia, pulled her up and placed her safely behind him. Veturia held him tight and did not loosen her grip until they reached the villa. Workers and servants alike whispered and giggled while the two changed into proper festival attire in separate bedrooms. Publius had left earlier to return to

Neapolis for supplies. That left Parosius with no one to question his dress code or to make sport of his sudden high social standing. Acknowledging his lack of social etiquette he reasoned that it didn't matter. He was going to spend the day with Veturia and nothing else would be an issue. Meeting in the vestibulum, Parosius looked deep into Veturia's beautiful brown eyes and his uncharacteristic nervousness melted away. He held her hand as they settled into the awaiting coach.

Arriving just outside of town they left their driver and coach at a large stable. Vehicles were not allowed on the streets of Herculaneum; only horses walked by their owner could venture onto the roads. After freeing one of the coach horses from its harness, Parosius grasped Veturia gently around the waste and placed her on it. From there he walked the steed to a small stable near their party's destination. Walking together to the forum, Veturia demonstrated her ability to communicate without taking a breath, while Parosius his capacity to listen.

The forum was the gathering place for the town's people and today was no different. It was much smaller and less crowded than the forum of Rome, and for that reason, more relaxing. In Rome, most of the men talked of politics or business, and the woman discussed social events and family. Here, in the center of Herculaneum, they spoke of vacations, relaxation, and interior decorating ideas. Slaves had no time or inclination to stop and carry on such discussions. Their daylight hours were always filled with hard labor. Parosius and Veturia strolled down the roads and visited the many shops. The forum was the scene of a weekly market where dickering was the sport. The people they met along the way appeared lighthearted, friendly, and soothing in manner and speech, unlike many who crowded the forum of Rome.

It would be hours before they were to attend the party. This gave them time to visit one of the public baths. They watched each other disappear past massive walls that divided the men from the women. The hot and cold pools felt good on their sweaty bodies. More time was spent in the sauna and then another quick dip in the cool water. Slaves made sure that they received every comfort. After being toweled off, they dressed and reunited at the entrance. Continuing to take in the sights, they came upon a diner that served a mid-day luncheon. After partaking of bread, fruit, nuts, and olives, they took a leisurely walk. Seeing young children playing in the back of a building brought Parosius back to his own childhood.

Cornelius was four years younger than Parosius, but even at seven he had been enterprising. Parosius remembered when he had seen his young brother spending much of his time building tiny wooden chariots. When Cornelius asked him for help to capture a dozen mice his curiosity peeked. "You'll see," is all he'd say. The young boy thought it would be profitable if he set up a mini-circus tempting the other boys to place bets on his mouse chariot races. He thought if the grown-ups could do it, why not them. He was right. He took in ten percent of every bet. He came home with some money, but mostly food. The tiny chariot races were not the only money making schemes Cornelius devised. His brother was the biggest boy in the neighborhood. The older boys liked to play a game called *Troy*. A group of about six boys would attempt to drag another across a line. Although the inevitable crossing would always take place, it was how long it took that made the game interesting. Pushing, pulling, and tackling were the only methods allowed. Once the gang got you down on the ground, it was just a matter of time before the average boy would be dragged across. Cornelius challenged that a colored stone could be thrown by anyone wanting to place a bet. His challenge was to retrieve the stone before his brother was dragged across the line. He invariably won his share, as Parosius proved to be a difficult opponent. As always, the proceeds would be split between the two brothers.

Veturia yanked on Parosius' arm bringing him back to the present. They continued walking hand-in-hand until they reached their final destination. As with the baths, women were separated from the men during dinner invitations. This ritual did not sit well with Veturia. She was welcomed to the home of Plautia Drusilla Asiaticus, wife of Gaius, to celebrate the Compitalia events with other women. This religious celebration praised their local gods, ancestors, and lares, but it was not without games and much, much wine. This part of the home was recently built for just such occasions.

Parosius was greeted by five fellow Romans at an adjoining door. His silver cup was filled with wine before he was all the way in. His host, Gaius Asiaticus, a round gregarious character, welcomed him and rushed him through the atrium and garden into a dining room where massive couches awaited the men. Parosius had built such homes in the past, but had never been invited to enjoy their splendor.

They raised their glasses to toast anything that entered their minds and at every conceivable opportunity. The men devoured the three-course meal, while conversation began to sound slurred and cloudy. Parosius' feeling of inadequacies among those of higher social standing or richer means began to fade away.

Gaius was a humorous man with a beard and head of hair so thick that it covered all of his face, save his eyes. The other four men were as diversified in stature as they were in knowledge. All had a trade that gave them unique expertise in their field—none more superior than the building profession of Parosius. The differences in bloodline and wealth mattered little to the men enjoying their wine.

As the hours waned, so did their ability to comprehend. While the others slumped into a stupor, Gaius invited Parosius to tour his admirable home. The murals were plentiful as were strategically placed statues. Two such statues of the goddess Diana stood on either side of the atriums pool, with her hands raised to the sky. Gaius and Parosius stood before the goddess of the moon and sang an incomprehensible song, then continued the tour staggering from room to room. The house held many separate bedrooms and a large kitchen with two stone ovens. Tripping into the garden, Parosius nearly fell into a formidable statue of Hercules. The marble hero seemed to be in the same drunken state as the two mortals in front of him.

"I'll be back, my friend. My cup runs empty," Gaius mumbled as he went off to look for a servant.

The statue of Hercules was postured in such a way as to relieve himself. Parosius, too intoxicated to find an appropriate place to urinate, joined his childhood hero. Returning to the dining room, he filled his cup and wandered out, looking for his host. His unstable legs dropped him to the floor several times. The ability to regain his balance proved an increasing and sizable challenge. After fighting off the desire to remain horizontal, he resumed his search and meandered dizzily into a room on the opposite side of the garden. The room was dark except for a single candle on a mantle. Under the mantle a polished bronze bath tub sparkled from the dim lighting. A woman of dark complexion was with Gaius Asiaticus. They were embraced in the water, their clothes dropped in a heap at the base of the tub. Parosius' blurry vision recognized the woman as one of the slaves that had earlier served the party. He did not have the mental capacity to make an opinion on what he saw in his inebriated state, but it didn't sit right with him. It was time to leave.

Parosius wobbled all the way to the opposite side of the home and through the vestibulum. Poking his drunken head out the door, he took a deep breath of fresh air and staggered out to the road. There his feet betrayed him again and he dropped to the ground. Only moments later, Veturia ventured out from her celebration. Taking a few steps toward the villa of Asiaticus, she was about to call for Parosius when she tripped and fell over him.

"I'll take you home now, Veturia," Parosius said, still on his back, in a barely audible voice.

Veturia, now lying next to him, giggled, "I am not sure you can get up, much less take me home." Sitting up, she added, "For someone who doesn't fit in, it sure appears your party was pleasurable."

"We must do this again…soon," Parosius slurred.

"You may not feel that way tomorrow. Come on, help me get you up."

Veturia pushed, groaned, and pulled as much as she could, but the big man was too heavy a load. The best she could do was to prop him up against the outside wall of the villa. Upon hearing the commotion, Pautia Asiaticus opened her door and requested that they stay the night. "You are kind, but if you could help me get him to our coach I'm sure we'll be fine," Veturia said.

Pautia ordered a servant to retrieve a horse and said, "Better to ride to the stable than walk in his condition." She then left to find her husband to help in getting Parosius up. Parosius mumbled in protest, but was not heard. Moments later, Pautia could be heard screaming at Gaius—not pleased upon witnessing his sexual display with the slave girl.

Hearing the shouting, Veturia asked Parosius what the trouble might be. As their horse arrived he said hesitantly, "He...ah...may have been caught in an awkward situation."

"What do you mean?"

"Help me to the horse. The cool air has helped my disposition. We'll talk of Gaius later."

This time the roles were reversed as the mighty Roman straddled the steed with his head down to minimize the dizziness. Veturia walked her load in the hazy dew of early morning. Finally arriving at the stable, Veturia woke their driver and they were soon brought back to the villa. The fresh air began to sober Parosius and by the time they reached the villa's vestibulum, he was nearly walking on his own. Just past the villa's peristyle, Veturia sat him down in her oecus.

"I should not be here. Point me to my tent and I will drop there."

"You can stay here tonight. I won't be long," Veturia said, leaving him. Whispering to a servant as she walked, they disappeared and quickly returned. She handed him a goblet.

"My mother taught me how to cure almost anything. Drink it."

Parosius smelled the concoction and nearly retched before Veturia pushed the cup to his mouth, forcing him to gulp down all of it.

Parosius pushed the mixture away, spitting and wiping the remains off his face. Seconds later he was running for the outdoors, emptying everything inside of him just outside the villa.

Returning to Veturia, "That was the most putrid and vile medicine I've ever tasted. What was that?"

"It is a family recipe. I'm not at liberty to divulge the secret. Besides—it did what it was supposed to do."

Veturia handed Parosius a towel and encouraged him to clean himself. She whistled happily as she went to her own bedroom. Returning expectantly back to where she left Parosius, she had changed into a thin, silk gown and rubbed her body with perfumes and oils. Despite his state, she approached Parosius, sitting next to him and leaning over to deliver a kiss that had been long overdue. She was met with the sound of a husky snore. Veturia pushed him, pinched and prodded, but nothing would awaken this huge man she had now fallen in love with. She didn't know whether to be happy or angry. She raised his heavy legs onto the couch and covered him up. Standing over him she thought about striking him in the face in one more attempt to wake him, but instead she kissed his cheek and whispered a good-night.

Parosius and Veturia's love grew strong, but under the cloud of social defiance. Parosius purposely slowed the building process of the villa. Veturia helped by changing room plans over and over again. This was their only way to make sure they could be together. Veturia knew her father would not allow such a union unless Parosius had the money and the backing to hold a prestigious office in Rome. Despite the few moments they were able to connect, they became committed to each other.

During the heart of the winter winds of AUC 831, the villa of Veturius Fortunatus was finally completed. The entrance to the atrium was flagged on both sides by bright blue marble statues of the lare, *Rurales*, protector of the land. Inside and to the left stood proudly a muscular Hercules, the town's founder and protector of those on long journeys. To the right was Apollo, lord of all civilization. The Fortunatus family would not use the new vacation home until spring, but on this cold day Veturius Fortunatus knelt before his family's altar and paid homage to the gods, lares and penates. In a formal room called the oecus, just beyond the peristyle, a shrine was painted that depicted the Fortunatus family—Veturius, mother Livia, Veturia, Crescentius, and a few ancestors flanked by dancing lares. In a prayer room, just to the left, two pedestals stood before the villa's largest statues—as yet unfinished. Parosius' final orders were to set masterful traps and deterrents to hinder thieves during the family's absence. The ceremony began with Veturius and his family kneeling, while Parosius and Publius stood back looking on.

"From Jupiter to Hercules…and Venus to Apollo, keep safe this house and all who enter." Veturius turned to an opposite wall with a mosaic of the Egyptian goddess Isis. "Place thy grace on this fine villa, as well as on its creators, Parosius, Publius and their fine crew," Veturius intoned, looking back at his builders. Undraping a golden sheet that rested on his right shoulder, he placed it neatly on the altar. On top of the sheet he laid a plate of wine-soaked crust and crumbled cinnamon. He then stood and turned to hug his wife, daughter, and son.

Veturius' bay-front villa was a showplace indeed. Countless steps led to the sea. At the top was an inviting vestibulum leading to a glorious atrium. A shallow impluvium graced the center of the atrium. From the opening above, terra-cotta spouts sloped downward, dropping rainwater to the shallow pool below. The pool water then drained into a cistern below the great mansion. Surrounding the pool were four huge columns. On either side were three bedrooms. At the far end a tablinum was to house the master's family records and business affairs. This led to a masterful peristyle. This open courtyard housed a unique garden with an imposing colonnade around it. Veturius left no stone unturned on his search for imported plants, trees, and statues. The kitchen, storerooms, and entertainment areas were no less elaborate, including a private heated bath for family and friends.

With his work on the villa completed, Parosius returned home to continue his efforts on the great amphitheater. Veturia would devote her time into planning her future with Parosius.

VIII

Life in Rome was exciting and dangerous, laborious or leisurely, filled with hope or filled with dread—depending upon who you were and what position of the social order you held. Tragedy was most prevalent among the slaves, but not exclusive. The elite had their share of misfortune.

Veturius Fortunatus was a rich and powerful man as Roman noblemen go. He not only had the bloodline, but could back it up with his leadership and accomplishments. His military experience was not long and did not reach the status of heroic. It did, however, instill memories that he wished he could forget.

Near the end of his time with the Roman army he was given orders to lead his six auxiliary cohorts to follow up on the capture of a group of Jewish zealots called Sicarii on the mesa of Masada. The group took over and lived there for years during and after the Great Revolt. In AUC 825, Vespasian sent Flavius Silva and his Tenth Legion to take the summit. After seven months, of siege, the Roman army finally completed an earthen ramp, using Jewish slaves to build around the western side of the mountain. This prevented the Jews from rolling rocks down the hill on their own people as they worked. When it was clear the zealots had no hope of escape, Veturius was called to assemble his cohorts, join the Tenth Legion, charge the mesa, and reclaim Masada.

The day before Veturius gave orders to move, the Jews burned nearly all that the fortress held. Then the Jewish men killed their wives and children, before ending their own lives—Veturius estimated over nine hundred in all. They were defiant of Roman rule to the very end.

Veturius would never forget the bloodied bodies huddled near the center of the fortress. Many seemed to stare back at him as his men rambled through Masada. As his order to set up a site on which to burn the remains was being carried out, he uncovered a cistern in hopes of finding fresh water. Inside was a young boy, perhaps thirteen years of age. The boy's dark, frightened eyes spoke to Veturius' heart rather than his common sense. He reached for the boy's arm to retrieve him from the water. In the process, the boy swung his other arm around, yielding a short blade. Veturius raised his hand, blocking the attack. He quickly subdued the boy, removing his weapon. Holding the young Jew, a soldier arrived with pointed sword.

"Do not harm him. Find a place to keep watch over him. Perhaps there will be others."

There were others, but only two old women and four children survived.

With such episodes behind him, Veturius had hoped that the remainder of his time on earth be filled with quiet and a reasonable amount of happiness. But on a cold January morning, his life changed.

Veturius was preparing for a day at the basilica to discuss business with a number of his fellow senators. He called for his personal servant, Maurus, who always hovered nearby, available for his master's every whim. Veturius was not a difficult master with any of his slaves. He was generally well liked and cordial with all that knew him. This time, however, his calls to Maurus went unanswered. He searched the servant quarters to no avail. As he ordered his stable boy to look for Maurus, a scream rang out. His wife Livia sat in the empty bedroom of her son Crescentius—his bed left undone and his chamber pot unused.

"Someone has taken him! Someone has taken our son! You must find him, Veturius!" she said, weeping and holding his tunic to her breast.

Veturius ran out of the room and stopped abruptly. He thought of Crescentius, his only son, a young boy who has not lived his life. In time he was to rule over his vast businesses and properties. Who could have taken his son? He would pay handsomely any ransom that was asked, but very few clues were left behind...no notes...nothing broken...no struggle. The only items missing from his room were his underclothing, sandals, and the tools Parosius had given him to keep him occupied. The boy rarely left home without them. One was a small, collapsible measuring tool and the other a marker of sorts, filled with a white dye. He enjoyed doing measurements for Parosius and at times overdid it with the white dye.

It had to be someone Crescentius felt comfortable with...Maurus!, Veturius had retained Maurus for over five years now—after changing his name from Baruch and saving him from duty in the mines. The slave had become a different person than he who was found hiding in the drinking water of Masada. It was difficult, at first, to gain his trust, but Veturius believed he had won such trust— until now.

Weeks passed without a trace of Crescentius and Maurus. Veturius used his influence to have search parties sent to all corners of Rome, and elsewhere, but still nothing. The cold winter months were ending, and all hope of finding Crescentius alive was bleak at best. Veturius and Livia became even more protective of their remaining child. Veturia missed her brother, but it seemed as though her entire life was on hold and she could no longer stand to mourn for the dead. She was young and alive and needed to proceed with whatever the gods had in mind for her. It was time to approach her mother about Parosius.

Livia Agrippa Fortunatus was of grand Roman blood. Her ancestral line went back to a general by the name of Livilious Agrippa, who served under Publius Cornelius Sulla. A large parcel of land was the reward for his allegiants to Rome. Though Livia presented a quick wit, it was a wonder she could function at all—considering all the horrendous ailments that had befallen her. Whether her illnesses were real or not was up for speculation. Her daughter Veturia never knew her when she wasn't complaining of some grave affliction. The loss of her son only amplified the maladies.

"Veturia, send for the doctor. I'm not at all well. The summer months bring the morning heat. Veturia, do you hear me?" Livia asked, dragging herself from bed.

The Fortunatus villa in Rome was situated between the Caelian hill and the Via Tusculana. Livia searched through the large home, looking for her daughter, when she came upon her in the embrace of Parosius. She let out a muffled scream and shuffled in her white gown, retreating back to the comfort of her bed.

"Give me a few minutes with her. I am quite good at adjusting her mood," Veturia said to Parosius as she straightened her ruffled stola. She went after her mother, leaving Parosius behind.

Livia had pale skin and a dark, sick look around her eyes. Her hair appeared to be thinning, but a long brown wig hung on a stand in the corner of the room always ready to be thrown on. When she smiled her eyes grew big and bright, much like Veturia's, revealing a life still left to live. Near her bed was an old prescription from a doctor, written on papyrus. It read:

Use the ashes of a deer's antlers, the blood of an ass diluted with wine, or the first manure excreted by an ass foal after its birth. Use the quantity of a bean and mix with wine. This cures the disease within three days.

"Do not cause your father and me such heartache, Daughter. You know how I hate it when he is upset," Livia said pulling the covers to just below her eyes. "That man you were…ah…clutching, he is the builder, is he not?" Now dropping the sheet to show the smile on her face she said, "He is quite handsome."

"I love him, Mother. I wish to marry Parosius and bear his children. You…you can help me, Mother," she said, putting a hand on Livia's shoulder. "You can get him an office. You can put him in favorable light," Veturia said emphasizing her words in such a way as to make importance of her mother's social standing.

"I do have a certain amount of influence," she said scuply.

"You do, mother. Nothing could be a better cure for…, what do you have this time?"

She put her head in the palm of her hand. "It's just a touch of dysentery. I really need to abstain from oysters and lampreys. Now, about Parosius…it would be quite a deed to take an uneducated plebe such as Parosius and coax others to put him in office. Do you think he's up to it? Do you think I'm up to it?" Without waiting for an answer, she continued, "Oh, but it must be done in secret. Your father must never know. Even today, he continues to look for a suitable husband for you. He is a busy man, your father. This week he is doing business in Aricia. Who knows where he will be next. Your father is not very observant in household matters. I could likely do what you ask. What position were you thinking of for your Parosius?" Veturia was used to her mother's rapid-fire banter with barely a pause for air.

"I believe you are more than capable, Mother. The title of aedile would do nicely, don't you think? Managing the roads and the publics dole would make him happy. I'll talk to Parosius about your sponsorship, and perhaps we will begin as early as tomorrow." Veturia smiled and hugged her mother.

"This is all going rather fast, don't you think, Daughter?"

"Not at all, Mother—for every rise of the sun seems an eternity away from my love."

"Your affection for this man is strong. Does he reciprocate such love?"

"Parosius would wed me tomorrow if circumstances allowed. As it is, he understands my need for Father's approval."

"Then I will do what I can," Livia said as Veturia left the room.

Parosius was pacing the floor when Veturia returned. "Perhaps I should speak to her."

"No, she's resting now. Go home. Let a little time pass. Tomorrow I'll send for you and we can…talk."

"Will she speak to your father of what she saw?"

"I have no fear of that."

Convincing her mother to help in the search for proper sponsors and tutors for Parosius was not the problem. The difficulty lay in the mind of Parosius. A man such as Parosius, any Roman for that matter, could not be ordered or taught by a woman. Veturia would need to handle things in such a way as to make Parosius think of taking office himself, perhaps for a greater cause.

The next day Veturia sent a message to Parosius with her slave, Pladia. Such was the process needed to keep their relationship secret from others.

"I will not bow to the pressures of achieving a title. If that is the course needed, then let us leave Rome. I am who I am. I am the best builder in Rome. It is your father that needs to change, not I," a proud Parosius exclaimed.

"Of course, you're right. I only ask if an office position might be something that our children might aspire to someday. You are the master of building structures. What responsibility might you have the knowledge to manage?"

Rubbing his chin, Parosius stated, "I have often thought of running the city water-ways and providing for proper building laws. As the laws now stand, they are ridiculous and cumbersome for any builder to strike out on his own."

"Spurius Felix is the man who is in charge of such a thing. Does he not hold one of the patrician aedile positions here in Rome?"

Parosius raised his eyebrow and said, "Spurius knows nothing of a technical matter. His talk is baseless, like a meal without meat."

"Then it is settled. You will take the open publiccorum aedile office," Veturia concluded with a knowing grin. "You would be perfect for such a position. Once the senate hears you and they see who has knowledge and who doesn't, who knows what may follow."

Parosius looked at her with suspicion. "Now you're playing a game. I've little schooling and I know nothing of oration, history, and senatorial matters. How would I state my intent?"

"I've had a discussion with my mother and she respects you very much, Parosius. Her respect came with a promise to help us. She could mingle with those who are of influence. As far as your education, a rhetor could assist with your...concerns."

"Your rhetor would need to possess much patience with such a student.

Education was more my brother's interest. Quintilian, my paedagogue, was a Greek slave and taught me to write. My skills at speech are lacking. My father knew only how to build and use the sword. Like him, I'm better with my hands than with my mouth."

"I think you have a perfect mouth," Veturia said kissing him on the lips.

"You know what I mean."

Veturia made a circle around Parosius seductively as she ran her fingers through his thick blond hair. He could smell her fragrance and it began to excite him. "You are one of the smartest men I've known and you learn fast. I fear it is you who will need to be patient, not the teacher."

"What of your father?"

"He will be told of our plans when the time is right."

Parosius pulled Veturia into his arms. "You are not only beautiful, but cunning. If I were Veturius, I would be just as selective with a suitor."

"Some day I will give you such a daughter, as well as many sons. They will love you as I do now."

Parosius picked Veturia up and carried her to a large lectus. There, they made love. This was not the love of man with woman for reasons of duty and procreation. This was true and pure happiness. They were making a pact that no human could break. She would know his naked body and he would explore her full breasts and soft skin. They were each other's slaves. With her mother asleep in her room and her father away on business, the afternoon, as well as the passion they could no longer restrain, was theirs.

Political posturing was the rule for Livia. The social gatherings, combined with her new found purpose, brought life back to her. She began to look, as well as speak, with a healthier appearance. While Veturia and her mother's planning seemed to be following the road to success, their subject's classes were not. The rhetorician, Isaeus was hired to turn Parosius into the political master he was not. Isaeus was an aged man but no more elegant a tongue in all of Rome could match this polished speaker. The daily education in the borrowed office of Veturius Fortunatus turned into more of a confrontation than anything else. The only common thread between the two was their equal similarities to the mule.

"No self-respecting Roman of office would use such terms. Your prefatory remarks must be neat and agreeable. State your position clearly. Conclude forcibly. Again!" Isaeus ordered Parosius.

Removing his blade from the belt of his tunic, Parosius challenged, "No man orders me so. Stand and draw your weapon."

Isaeus put his hands over his face. "My weapon of choice is of the oratorical persuasion, and by the look of yours, mine is invariably sharper. You'll not win a position in front of the senate, nor in front of your own family, without the proper syllogisms. Now, please, again."

Parosius returned his blade reluctantly and read the speech before him. Within a few months, he would need to pen his own set of words and state his case for the position of aedile. It would take great fluency and choice of expression to win over the senators. His love for Veturia kept him on task. As another test, Parosius, Cornelius and their father Lusius were invited to a dinner held by the teacher.

The Tacitus family was to be wined and dined at the prestigious villa of Isaeus and such a meal was too rare for them to refuse. They left their horses to the care of a slave. Upon entering his home, Isaeus asked the crew, "Where is your toothpick and napkin?"

"Right here!" Lusius said digging his fingers in his mouth and wiping it on his tunic. His sons rolled with laughter.

"I now understand where my student acquired his great manners. Never mind, I'll provide you with the proper dinner etiquette. Parosius, I hear you attended a dinner in Herculaneum. I hope to show you how to conduct yourself properly this time!"

"You can mock me all you wish, Teacher. You could only wish to have as jolly a time as I had—the parts I remember, that is."

"Yes...well, follow me to the dining area and we'll begin," Isaeus said walking with head up and shoulders back.

The men lounged on sloping couches arranged in a U-shape around a central table. The dinner lasted for hours and included three courses. Slaves served their every need at the flick of Isaeus' finger. Shellfish and salad was followed by dove, and stuffed dormouse. The final course was a fresh supply of fruit. While watered-down table wine was available throughout the meal, the finest of wine arrived after their palates were full. At each interval, Isaeus would plead with his guest to follow all his etiquette rules. Written on wax tablets were inscribed; Keep your tongue civil—lustful glances at another man's wife is vulgar—if your napkin is not dirty, you are. Although Veturia and her mother concocted their plan with the best of intentions, it may have been ill advised with this horde. The Tacitus family marveled at the wave of food the slaves brought them. It was enough to last for weeks at the Tacitus home. Their manners, although crude, were kept in check right up until the heavy drinking began. Isaeus' studious demeanor began to loosen as he made an error in judgment and tried to match the same wine intake of his students.

As the evening went on, the appetizer—Flamingo tongues—were served. The now drunk and loud Isaeus took the first bite of the delicacy and quickly spit it out. His eyes turned accusingly toward the slave who had served him and immediately ordered him into the courtyard. There, he brandished a whip and reached back to punish the man. With his father and brother fast asleep, Parosius staggered behind his teacher and pulled the whip from him.

"This man ruined good food. He needs to be punished."

"It's late. I'm sure it was meant to be served earlier. Perhaps it toughened over the wait," Parosius reasoned.

"This is part of having a title, Parosius. I ordered that the meat be tender. You can't let up when a mistake is made," Isaeus said reaching for his whip.

Parosius looked hard at Isaeus and then at the slave. Shaking his head, he handed the whip back to his inebriated teacher. "I've made countless mistakes in my life, but because I am a Roman I bear no scars." Parosius woke his father and brother and gathered their things to leave.

"What rushes you so, Son?"

"I'm not pleased with how the teacher rules his people. But…yet, I am troubled. To interfere in another man's matters…" Parosius raised his eyebrow and ran to his horse to retrieve his sword, hustled back to the courtyard, where the slave cowered, crying loudly. Once again Parosius pulled the whip from Isaeus, swung his sword swiftly, and cut the flagellum in half, dropping it to the floor.

"You are a good teacher, Isaeus, but this lesson eludes me."

Isaeus suddenly began to clap as his slave turned and took several bows.

"Thank you, Patri. You should have been in the theater," Isaeus said to his slave, as he wiped a red substance from the back of his servant—an ad hoc thespian. "Now go see to your kitchen duties."

"You…this was…," Parosius puzzled.

"I can teach you manners and grammar, but character is another matter. You've passed the test. Rome should consider itself fortunate to honor you with office."

Parosius left his teacher with the confidence he needed, along with an unexpected friendship.

IX

The amphitheater was beginning to look magnificent. Occasionally the slaves and other laborers revolted at the conditions and severity of the work before them. Hundreds died from the hazards of the work, be it accident, exhaustion, or punishment. With most of the heavy work done, much less life was lost. While Parosius managed the overall structure, several supervisors were in charge of keeping the workers on task. On most occasions, slaves who did not perform were punished swiftly and harshly. Parosius and Cornelius did not support such tactics. They picked their battles and intervened when possible. As tough as the work was at the amphitheater, it was nothing compared to the rock quarries. The digging, removal, and cutting of the rock was merciless labor. Slaves were beaten and the work was without end. Those that were fit enough, prayed for the privilege of working in the amphitheater, or to be selected as a gladiator. The time was near when the Emperor would order the collection and training of a larger troupe of gladiators for the amphitheater's grand opening. Compared to the quarry, being a gladiator induced a feeling of being free, though that freedom might be short-lived.

The cruelty of man can sway a life like the wind. A changing event at the age of eleven had left Parosius and his young brother with memories of more than their share of human suffering.

The city prefect, Pedanius Secundus, had 225 slaves in his charge. In the dark of night, Pedanius had been killed by one of his own slaves. The killer was a male cook who fell in love with the same young man as Pedanius had used for his own sexual pleasures. Pedanius had promised the cook his freedom upon payment of 350 denarii. The cook's plan was to leave with the young man as soon as he was free. When Pedanius learned of the cook's love for the young man, he raised the amount to 500 denarii. Each day the anger grew inside the cook until he finally snapped, cutting into his master with a butcher's knife. Roman law required that should a free man be murdered by one of his slaves, *all* of his slaves could be executed. The Roman Senate discussed the case and decided that all 225 slaves were to be crucified. The majority of senate members agreed that this sentence should prevent future slave plots and encourage slaves to report any suspicious plots to their master. Others argued that too many innocent lives would be lost. The majority rule prevailed.

In a large, open field Parosius stood beside Cornelius and a childhood friend, Dasius. Their young friend was the son of slave parents who were among those suffering on the cross. The boys didn't know the reason for such a massive display of horrible and painful death, but they understood the power that Roman rule held over those that were not free. The Tacitus family took Dasius into their home, where he stayed until he was old enough to take care of himself. Never able to erase the memory of his innocent mother and father dying before him, he eventually took his own life. Parosius and Cornelius might have ended their own lives much the same way, had it not been for the teachings of their father, as well as their mother before she died. "You can do more by picking your fights on your own terms than by rebelling against all odds," Lusius would say. Though very young Parosius still recalled his mother saying, "You can't change things if you're dead." These words became the Tacitus creed. The boys remembered and learned.

Word was circulating about Parosius Tacitus and his run for office. While supervising the placement of a marble fountain near a south amphitheater entrance, a sweaty Parosius heard footsteps.

"I've heard of your plans and am disheartened, Parosius," the crusty Veturius Fortunatus said forcibly, his daughter shadowing him.

"You are in disagreement with my...plans? Even of those with..."

"Mother...yes, my father is aware of the help you've received from mother," Veturia broke in with no time to spare as she had stepped out from behind.

"I hear you've grown a taste for office, Parosius. Would not I be the first of whom you would seek for help in such matters? Why should I be the last to know of your plans?"

"Forgive me...I didn't want to...ah...bother you with my personal pursuits.

"What bother? It would be my pleasure to help where needed," Veturius said while turning toward Veturia. "Daughter, this is not a place for women. Did I not leave you to care for your mother?"

"She's taken a turn for the better. Besides you've forgotten your flask and I've brought it to you. In this heat, you must thirst." Veturia lied.

"Well, let's have it... then away with you."

Looking at her hands Veturia continued the ruse, "In my haste I seemed to have forgotten it myself."

"Parosius, the girl is a bit off, but she is my daughter. Could you take a break from your work and escort her back to my home? As for your aspirations, I expect you to come to me with your needs from now on. Is that understood?"

"It is, my Lord," Parosius said bowing his head.

"No need for such formalities now, Parosius, you'll soon be of great status."

"Thank you, my...thank you," Parosius stammered. He quickly relayed orders to have a coach. The driver approached the two lovers as Parosius helped Veturia into the back covered carrier. This was the first time Parosius was ever inside such a coach and it took him a moment to take in such plush surroundings.

"Your father may be of great help to me politically, but will he be as gracious about our union?"

"You nearly found out only moments ago," Veturia joked.

"This will not be the last time you will need to repair what my words destroy, Veturia."

"Don't be hard on yourself, Parosius. There are many who should never speak—what pours out can only be used for sleep. It is for your words I live," Veturia said lovingly over the noise of the coach wheels as they clanged against the stone road, which vied with the daily chatter of the customers and shop owners on either side of the road. Both took in the smells they grew up with in the busy center of Rome. The fragrance of fresh fruit, bread baking on a large hearth, and bottled oils and olives filled the air. As quickly as it takes to turn one's head they were overcome by the aroma of a cloth maker and fish seller. When they reached home, Parosius helped her from the coach and kissed her gently.

Veturia looked to the sky and said, "It will be a while before the sun drops."

"There is something brewing inside that mind of yours...what is it, Veturia?"

"I like the races. Could you take me there?"

"Your father made a request to bring you home, and I accepted."

"And so you shall...eventually."

Rome featured several race tracks. The largest, the Circus Maximus, could entertain as many as 250,000 spectators including those who stood on the adjoining hills. It was located in the valley between the Palatine and Aventine hills. Most men enjoyed the shear bravery and life-ending crashes of the races, but the women preferred to pick their favorite driver and cheer him on. The first race of the day was also the featured race. Four factions, each with their own color— Red, White, Blue, and Green—would face off in a race against speed, thirteen sharp turning posts, and their opponents. Today, Veturia knew her favorite was racing in the feature. Although her father did not approve of her betting on her hero, she would bet just the same.

"We'll need to hurry—Scorpus begins in a short time."

"Scorpus," Parosius muttered silently.

"He's won over 2,000 times for the green, you know—well over 30,000,000 sesterces in prize money."

Parosius knew that all winnings went to the faction owners. Scorpus was a slave and would likely stay a slave, but he was treated as a hero wherever he raced and to him it was worth the danger.

Veturia's status allowed her to sit with Parosius in the first tier. They arrived as the introductory procession was nearly concluded. Around the track, carriages held statues of gods and spectators applauded their favorite deities. The god Victory led the parade—its carriage filled with palm branches. Young boys ran to the carriage and, gathering the palms, threw them to the spectators. Whenever a favored driver won his race, a spectator would toss her palm to the victor. The parade marched on, and Victory was followed by Mars, Phoebe, Bacchus, Castor, and finally Venus—each god a possible patron saint for those in attendance. As the procession was escorted off the track, Spurius Felix, the Aedile of Rome spoke briefly. "My friends, welcome to the best races in the world. Let the races begin!"

This was a single-entry race, meaning one entry per color. In a triple-entry race you would have three of each color racing. Races were usually run with two, three, or four-horse chariots. Today's feature was a four-horse event. The chariots were small and flimsy, the turns tight, and the driver's cutthroat.

Scorpus waved to his green faction fans and awaited the sudden toot of the trumpet. No teams for this one, just a flat-out race between each faction to the finish. Scorpus was bare-chested except for a lone strap. With his whip in hand, the city's hero looked confident and strong, yet his actual size was small, consistent with that of most drivers. The faction owners liked their drivers light, but flexible. Each starting gate was staggered to allow for the same distance of travel to the first turn.

Trumpets blared as the grooms let go of their horses and the driver whipped them into action. The chariots were weightless in comparison to the strong and speedy steeds in front. Scorpus looked surprised to see he was not in the lead, but continued confidently. The seven-lap race reached the first of thirteen dangerous turns when the brightly painted red chariot burst into the lead. Thus began a game of cutting off any chance for an opponent to pass him. Scorpus took his time and dealt with the charging blue challenger. His chariot in the air more than on the ground, he sharply cut across the track on the inside. This swung his chariot into the side of the blue-faction, pushing them into the far wall. The 'blue' driver was immediately raised into the air by the sudden crash, his chances of survival remote, at best, as the white team trampled him. This, in turn, slowed the white-faction severely and made it a two-man race. Through each lap and nearly every turn the two locked up and used their whips savagely on each other. The dust now covered the air and breathing became an after thought. Scorpus held back just far enough to stay within striking distance. The short straight-away in the seventh and final lap would be his only chance to pass his opponent. Scorpus leaned forward— toes stretched against the floorboard. As he pulled even with the 'red' driver, both stopped whipping and screaming at their horses and turned their whips on each other. Flesh ripped open and the heavy dust was now mixed with blood. Scorpus reached with his dripping forearm and caught his opponent's whip. Surprised by the sudden pull, the 'red' driver lost his balance and fell to the side of his chariot, holding on to the floorboard with one hand. Finally he lost his grip, fell hard to the ground, and rolled quickly to the far wall, just missing the oncoming white chariot. Moments later, palm branches were tossed at the feet of the winner, Scorpus.

Veturia stared admirably at the victor. She raised her palm branch to throw it, but it was snatched up by Parosius. Feeling jealousy for the first time in his life, he snapped the branch in two. He saw disappointment in Veturia's eyes.

"Can you admire another man and still love me?"

"I praise the driver's skill, I love and admire you."

Parosius looked down at the broken palm branch and handed Veturia a fresh one to throw at the feet of Scorpus.

With the day still young, Veturia was still in an adventurous mood. She convinced Parosius to take her for a leisurely ride north before going home. The ride on the Via Flaminia took them to the well serviced groves and walkways on the Tiber bank, not far from the Mausoleum of Augustus. Spring flowers were beginning to bloom. Veturia voiced her frustrations of separation to Parosius. As they discussed their futures, they scarcely noticed that their path had grown narrower from the abundance of trees and overgrowth. The sun was now showing itself sporadically through the branches. Parosius utilized his sword wheeling it at the thick branches. Veturia looked at the strange sword in fascination. With a sharp blade on one side and jagged teeth on the other, it was not typical.

"Where did you get such an odd weapon?" she asked.

"It was a gift from my father. He believes the sword to hold some kind of special strength."

"Tell me its story."

Sitting back, he said, "Very well, but you must keep its secret to yourself."

He waited for Veturia to nod in agreement. "When I was a boy my father told me that a Christian of some note was held in the tullianum dungeon."

"I don't think I've ever known a Christian. Are they not vile creatures?" Veturia interrupted.

"Like slaves, it depends on who it is. This one was high in their order. My father was commissioned to repair a prison vault. At the time Father was well known for his building knowledge and was beginning to advance in status and wealth. The Christian was there for a long time and awaited his fate upon the return of Nero from Athens. At first my father despised the man and his beliefs, but his words grew interesting. One day, as the man's health worsened and Nero was only days from his return, my father did something he was soon to regret. He felt pity on the man and left the door unlocked. The man walked past the sleeping guards and escaped, as if taking a stroll to the baths."

"What of your father after the Christian was found missing?" Veturia asked.

"Eventually he was charged with allowing the prisoner to escape. The case against him was without evidence, but he was charged just the same. With Nero's return, he was summoned. As an angry Nero was about to sentence Father to take the place of the escaped prisoner and be put to death on the cross, the Christian returned. He explained that it was he that forced the door open and that my father had nothing to do with it. Nero let my father go, but let it be known that he was never to be accepted as more than a simple builder and paid accordingly."

"What of the sword?"

"Before the man was crucified, he asked my father if he would see a woman, his daughter. I believe her name was, Petronilla. He was to retrieve the sword from her and keep it as his own. It was to be a small reward for being kind to the Christian. The holy man said it would help him in his life's journey. He claimed it had a long history. My father retrieved the sword and kept it, only taking it with him on occasion."

Parosius looked at the well kept weapon thoughtfully. "It was given to me on my twelfth year."

Veturia smiled and felt a warm feeling of security sitting next to Parosius and his unique amulet.

Parosius, enjoying his time with Veturia, noticed an odd mark on one of the trees. He stopped and stepped off the coach to have a better look. A few feet into the thicket, he noticed another branch with the same marking. Veturia followed, puzzled by his behavior. Parosius recognized the marking as similar to the builder's dye he had given Veturia's brother Crescentius to keep him busy before his disappearance. They followed a trail leading deeper and deeper into a wooded area and finally came upon the very edge of the Tiber. The area was thick with brush, and they found it difficult to move. Hearing a scream, Parosius hurried toward the noise. Stopping at the river's bank he again unsheathed his sword, pushing tree branches aside. He backed up suddenly upon the sight of Veturias' brother. His wounds were fresh and appeared to be fatal. He stood angrily and heard another scream. This time he recognized it as Veturia.

He ran madly, following the screams, and stopped at a small open field. There, Veturia was held by several men, each with markings at the neck revealing them as Jewish slaves.

"Maurus…why?" cried Veturia.

"Did your father not tell you of his time as a Roman officer? My father, mother, sister…all dead…at the hands of his soldiers," Maurus replied, his voice stammering. He held a tall spear that dripped of her brother's blood.

"Let her go, Maurus. You've had your revenge."

"We will never recover what was taken from us," another slave shouted as he pointed his own spear on Veturia.

Parosius stood much bigger than the three slaves that held Veturia, but a charge might have caused her harm.

"Do you think killing a young boy makes you a man, Maurus?"

"The name, Maurus, died the day I escaped your Roman laws. I am Baruch, a man—not a slave. Crescentius would have lived had he not yelled out. I had no choice."

Veturia cried out her brothers name, but was muffled by the hand of her captor.

"If you are such a man, fight me for Veturia's freedom," Parosius challenged.

The other slaves mocked the Roman and cheered on their comrade.

"Drop your sword," Baruch ordered. "Throw him a spear. We'll see who the greater man is."

Baruch wasted no time and lunged at Parosius before he was given the spear. Blocking the attempt, Parosius reached for his sword and forced it down on Baruch's spear snapping it in two pieces. In less than a second, Parosius thrust his weapon deeply into Baruch's stomach. He then turned the sword to the slave that held Veturia tossing it through the air into the slave, hitting him in the middle neck, just missing Veturia. The remaining slave ran into the woods, escaping certain death at the hands of Parosius. Free of her captors,

Veturia embraced Parosius and, gathering herself asked, "Did Maurus hurt my brother?"

Parosius hung his head and showed her where Crescentius' body lied. Veturia ran to her brother. As she knelt she found not a bloodied death, but a body struggling to hold onto life. She called Parosius to quickly carry her young brother to the coach. Crescentius' hands still clutched a marker and a small wooden measure.

Veturius thanked Parosius for finding his son and warned all that were present that the name of 'Maurus' was never to be spoken in his presence again. For Crescentius his recovery was long, difficult, but fully realized.

X

If he were approved as aedile, Parosius would be charged with the public works of buildings, roads, grain allotment, and the aqueduct system. The position no longer required leadership concerning gladiator games and other entertainment such as chariot racing, as in earlier times. While most Romans thought the games of the gladiators an exciting diversion to a sometimes rough existence, Parosius found it cruel and uncivilized. He believed that the harsh discipline dealt to slaves in the working world was unavoidable and, at times, necessary. But to force slaves and criminals to practice the sport, and then use what they've learned to slaughter each other, did not sit right with him. To be used in cases of criminal justice was understandable—to those who volunteered because wages could not be found elsewhere was a matter only the gladiator could decide—but to force an untrained slave to enter into a fight that was a highly unfavorable match, whether human or beast, was blood sport.

Cornelius watched as his big brother dressed in preparation of his maiden political engagement. Parosius pushed his drab wool tunic aside and reached for an artificially whitened toga, the very garment that Livia had picked out for his presentation to the senate. In office, he would receive a rich white tunic with a purple border.

"What have you done with my brother?"

"Leave me be, Cornelius. I can scarcely keep from shaking as it is. I beg of you, come to the court with me and back your big brother."

"Why is it that all of Rome believes you a capable man, but the man himself thinks himself a buffoon? You'll be fine. You wouldn't want me to turn down an invitation from an important Pompeian citizen, would you? What a political mistake that would be. Besides, it's not all pleasure. Do you not want me to collect more details on their arena?"

"Yes, I need the measurements, but that can wait. I hardly think an invitation from Samius could be a tool for political positioning. But go! Have your fun...within reason."

"Samius and I are old friends and he's as gracious and responsible as any...drunk I know." Leaving, he continued, "May your discussions be as wise as your convictions, my lord," Cornelius said, bowing mockingly to Parosius.

"And may you fall off your horse and break your...," whispered Parosius as he watched his brother leave.

The senators gathered on the first floor under arched niches. In the rectangular basilica, two stories high, light shown down from the clerestory above. A well known orator and historian by the name of Gaius Plinius Secundus stood before the group. He was the respected author of a 77-volume encyclopedia of natural history and an admiral of a Roman fleet. This was not a criminal court, but Pliny called the senators to order just the same. Rome filled four aedile positions, as well as many more for other cities. It was not unusual to discuss a candidate before assigning a location for the position.

The senate members wore the proper white gown with purple sash and sat quietly as Pliny was about to begin. Parosius' nomination was the first order of business that morning. Although

Pliny had never met Parosius, he announced Parosius as if he had the ability to walk on water. Pliny had agreed to praise the young man in a one-hand-washes-the-other agreement with Livia Fortunatus.

"Friends, how many times are we subjected to the pleas of a man seeking office? He is presented as an honest, trustworthy man who has the background of education and the experience brought to him by bloodline leadership. I present to you today a different type of man, but no less capable. You will recognize Parosius Tacitus by the work he has done throughout Rome and beyond. Look no farther than the villa of our own Veturius Fortunatus in Herculaneum. If you need more proof of his ethics and abilities, see the palace of Vespasian, who is currently ill and to whom we all wish a fast recovery." Pliny stopped for a moment to force some cheers from the crowd. "Finally, the nearly completed Flavian Amphitheater is managed by none other than Parosius Tacitus. This is a man who is not only honest and trustworthy, but who demonstrates how our Roman Empire creates and inspires. If this sounds like a plea for the position of Aedile, you are right. As for me, I do not question whether Parosius Tacitus is right for the office, only where the position would be assigned. Today, my friends, I give you Parosius Tacitus."

From the rear, a surprise guest entered. Emperor Vespasian approached the center. The consul of Rome was greeted with great applause, despite those in attendance who did not favor him. His age was beginning to show as he weakly moved to his bench.

"I would hope your generous applause was for my friend, Parosius Tacitus, and for his magnificent introduction our scholarly colleague, Pliny—for it is Parosius that is of discussion today." Slowly making his exit, he continued, "I've duties to attend to...I will leave you. What you have heard from Pliny is what you hear from me. He is a good and knowledgeable man. Do what is right." Having said what he wanted, the emperor left the court but not without a wink of an eye towards Parosius.

Given that Pliny had already driven home most of the speech Parosius had memorized, he merely complemented the orator and added a few choice words of his own. Despite his nervousness and the sweat that poured from his forehead, he gave an admirable oration. The vast majority of senators were in boisterous favor of both the Pliny speech and Parosius. His teacher, Isaeus, stood at the entrance and nodded to his pupil before leaving the gathering. There were a few whose patrician blood did not allow them to give favor, even for the office of a plebe. One of them was the current patrician aedile, Spurius. After a short discussion, it was decided that Parosius would be a favorable candidate for Rome's plebeian aedile. This one year term would begin after formal documents were drafted. The position could lead to many things, one of which could be changing his status from plebian to the equestrian order.

As Parosius stood to greet and thank the Roman elite for his introduction to office, a slave interrupted with an urgent message. Written on a papyrus, it read:

Brother, I've been arrested. My trip did not turn out as I'd hoped. Pompeii is an interesting place with many women who seem to enjoy my company. One in particular didn't mention the status of her husband. Please hurry! Cornelius.

Parosius apologized to the senate members and quickly made his exit from the chambers. After giving his father the good and bad news of the day, he and Publius set out for Pompeii. Parosius had just finished a successful campaign in front of the senate of Rome and his life was beginning to change rapidly. He wasn't sure he liked the path his life was taking, but if an office was what it took to spend his nights with Veturia, then so be it. Once he helped his brother out of yet another irresponsible crisis, he would return to Rome and begin his new life.

On the south end of the forum stood Pompeii's imposing Basilica. The structure served as a combination law court, bank, and meeting place for politics and business. Cornelius had been placed in a hearing room in back of the building. Across the street were twelve dark prison holding cells. Prisoners were not there to fill out life sentences. Such cells were temporary living spaces for those sentenced to be condemned, banished, or sent to the games as meals for the beasts. Parosius and Publius arrived from Rome in just over two days. They could hear the vulgar banter of prisoners waiting for their punishments to be doled out. Parosius wondered if his brother's next home would be in those cells. As it was, the hearing room he was placed in was not much better.

"Cornelius! You've finally purchased your own place," Parosius said in an attempt to humor his brother.

"I don't mean to boast but it is quite nice. Publius, you've come to see the place as well."

"It's dreary and deplorable. Not unlike your situation," Publius noted.

Cornelius sat in a stone cell with a tiny opening in the back and a door with large wooden bars from top to bottom. He'd been there for nearly a week.

"Your timing is impeccable, Cornelius. Did you know your brother is about to become something of an elites?" Publius asked.

"I had little doubt. Congratulations, big brother," Cornelius said stretching his arm through the barred door. "Did you know that they had four magistrates in Pompeii and one of them is married to a very beautiful woman?"

"You didn't!"

"Well, yes, I did. I didn't know she was married, but I do now. She was more than willing, and I was in the giving mood."

"You're always in the giving mood, brother. What was this wonderful woman's name?" Parosius asked.

"Mucia—kind of rolls off your tongue and drips like sweet nectar, doesn't it?"

"I hope she was worth it because you can bet she'll say whatever her magistrate husband tells her to say in court," Publius interjected.

"I'm going to need someone who can stand in court and turn a good phrase, won't I?"

"You are going to need someone who can turn a day's worth of phrases," Parosius prophesied.

Rubbing his chin with a look of uncharacteristic seriousness, Cornelius asked, "Do you have anybody in mind?"

"I do. I tried to get the best, but none were available under such short notice. Quintus Tullius Martius is his name. He comes highly recommended."

Publius looked down with a smirk.

"Recommended by whom, Brother?"

"By our bank accounts—I'm afraid he's all that father and I could afford."

Parosius and his father got just what they paid for in acquiring the services of one Quintus Tullius Martius. The portly man was a blowhard of the highest order. He was not without some talent, but after all, it was Quintus against all of Pompeii. In short order Cornelius was charged with adultery. The trial was held in Pompeii. It proceeded quickly. The magistrate, Decimus Stuvius, whose wife was the *victim,* hired a prosecutor who did not have the eloquent tongue of Quintus, but made his points decisively and without fanfare. Being in his home court was all that he needed.

Stuvius was a squirrel of a man. Although his life's record showed military devotion and accomplishment, most of what was attributed to him during past wars was highly exaggerated. He had grown to be a blood-thirsty zealot during daylight hours and a man prone to perversions at night. He pushed to see Cornelius punished under the guise of honor for his wife.

The punishment, if found guilty, was flogging and crucifixion for slaves, banishment to an island or to gladiator school for freedman, free man, or plebian. For those of patrician blood, it was a slap on the hand.

All weapons were left at the door as the court attendees entered the Basilica. Cornelius stood before the court, his wrists tethered together and a length of chain connecting them to his bound ankles. Quintus Tullius Martius stood next to his client. When Cornelius turned to face the court of twenty men they seemed taken aback by the sight of this large, handsome man with the whitest of smiles. This did not fit the typical scoundrel that appeared before them. Decimus Stuvius reached toward Cornelius in an almost staged attempt to avenge his wife. He was only half the size of the accused and while his fellow Pompeian's pulled him back he shouted, "If I had my weapon you'd be dead." After order was restored, the prosecutor, Asinius Rufus, began with the prosecution.

"Distinguished members of the court! The man before you is a despicable character. Through witnesses and the written record of the victim, I will prove that that vile being forced himself on the righteous woman, *Mucia,*" he intoned pointing to the young, shapely wife of Decimus Stuvius, who was now being held by her husband. Her eyes were adorned with thick, light-blue makeup, covering what appeared to have been blackened by her abusive spouse. She wore a long gown that matched her eye make-up in color. She turned to look at Cornelius and quickly buried her head into Stuvius' bony chest.

Asinius had little trouble questioning the three men who claimed to have been at the dinner party that included Mucia and her new acquaintance, Cornelius of Rome. Having rehearsed their lines and collected a monetary reward for their time from Stuvius, they all had the same story.

The witnesses claimed Cornelius had taken a liking to Mucia and had spent much of the night in close discussion with her. When asked where Stuvius was, they claimed her husband was busy attending to an ill friend. As the party-goers started to leave, Cornelius had picked up the helpless Mucia and carried her to a guest bedroom. They heard the victim scream and make attempts to get free, but knew it was fruitless for someone so small to fight off the big man. When asked why they had not come to the woman's aid, they said,

"We tried to get up, but were too drunk to move. It's possible the man from Rome put something in our drink."

The prosecutor then read from the victim's version of what happened. Because women were not allowed to speak inside the Basilica, he read from a scroll.

"I met the man (Cornelius) after having been invited to a dear friend's dinner party. He appeared to be an interesting man, but as I began to say my farewells, he insisted I stay. I told him my husband would be worried, but he insisted once more. As I turned to leave, he picked me up and placed me on his shoulder and carried me into a guest room. There, despite my screams, he did unspeakable things. Having fulfilled his needs, he made his leave. Not finding an escort sober enough to take me home, I ran to the safety of my home and my husband. He immediately summoned soldiers to have the man found. That is all I have to say."   *Mucia Stuvius*

Asinius looked up from the scroll and glared once more at Cornelius. "As I said,…vile. I can barely look at him." He walked away slowly and sat down, giving the floor to Quintus.

Clapping his hands, Quintus applauded his rival and said, "Quite a performance. It had everything you need to convict a man— except accuracy. Let me tell you about this "vile" man. He's worked all day and most nights for as long as he can remember constructing an amphitheater such as Rome has never seen. He didn't take weekends off to lounge at his villa. He only dreamt of one day owning such a place. After years of constant and loyal service, he was asked to make measurements of your fine arena and return after a visit to a friend's party. On invitation, he visited his friend, Samius, and happened upon the lovely Mucia Stuvius. She extended a warm welcome by enticing him to follow her to a dinner party." Quintus paused and walked back to where his client was sitting and took a drink of water. His pudgy face was sweating profusely. "I, myself am not so strong that I don't occasionally give in to temptation. Sometimes, I listen to comedies and attend performances of mimes when I should be visiting my wife's relatives. Moreover, I laugh, jest and find ways to amuse myself…after all, I am a man. But, should an attractive woman such as Mucia Stuvius invite and then spend time with me, I—like any of you—would be flattered and most interested. My client stands by his claim that he was not given any information concerning Mucia Stuvius' marital status and was enticed into what happened later in the night. Worried that her husband would think her a whore, she cries rape."

Quintus called one of the three witnesses who had previously testified.

"I recall our poor victim's written…ah…story about how you were not sober enough to escort her home. I also recall your own testimony on how you were too drunk to move and you thought the Roman may have tampered with your drink. Does that sound right?"

The witness nodded.

Quintus turned and looked at the court. "Am I the only one here that finds it odd that the same witnesses—admittedly inebriated beyond the point of movement—still had the presence of mind to recall detailed facts about what they think may have happened in a room far from their own?" He paused for effect and looked at the faces in the court room one more time before turning to wink at Cornelius, as if to say "we have them" as he sat down.

It took all of five minutes for the partisan court to find Cornelius guilty. In the end, Quintus gave the court a stern look and left their presence knowing there was nothing to be done. He would bring his argument to Rome, but here in Pompeii the ruling went in favor of their own. No amount of evidence was going to change their minds.

Parosius appealed to anyone who would listen, but his pleas fell on deaf ears. Cornelius' sentence was swift, and he was quickly ordered to train as a gladiator. He was required to fight at least three times a year for three years. Should the unlikely event occur that he last that long, he would once again be free.

Returning to Rome, Parosius made an attempt to ask a favor of the Emperor, but was met with more bad news. Emperor Vespasian's health took a turn for the worse. Parosius rushed to be by his side. Vespasian's family allowed Parosius to say goodbye to the great emperor. Bowing past Vespasian's mistress, Caenis, his sons, Titus and Domitian, and Titus' beautiful young daughter, Julia Flavia, he reached the bed of Vespasian. Julia, having never seen Parosius before, smiled as he passed. Her smile remained despite the mournful occasion.

Looking up to see his young builder, the Emperor, ever the humble soldier, made one last dig at the folly of his title. "Parosius, how good of you to say farewell to an old man. Alas, I think I'm turning into a God," he said, referring to the penchant of his predecessors to elevate their status to that of a god. He would die later that day on June 23rd, AUC 832. Vespasian had fought to have his sons succeed him as emperor and he won that argument. His son Titus was declared the new Emperor of Rome.

Titus Flavius Vespasianus was a victorious war hero during the Jewish rebellion that ended with the sack of Jerusalem nine years earlier. His career took him away from Rome much of the time. As Emperor, he would need more time to satisfy his position in the senatorial order. Like his father, he was a down-to-earth type of man who laid great stock on reasoning powers.

Parosius felt sure he could reason with Titus, despite his tendency towards a quick temper. He thought that with luck he could win an early release for his brother. How the change of emperors would affect his plight for office was difficult to judge.

XI

Sent to the largest training facility in Rome, the *Ludus Maximus*, Cornelius would have less than two weeks to prepare for his first fight. His event was to be held in the town where all his troubles began, Pompeii. The gladiators traveled from town to town. A manager would own a troupe of them. Such a man rented the past prisoners of war, slaves, and criminals out to whoever cared to stage games. Not all gladiators held such backgrounds—as many as fifty-percent were free men who volunteered. They signed up to a five-year contract, thereby giving up their freedom, but money was money. Cornelius was under the tutelage of Scaurius, a toothless man whose back was covered with hair, and yet none rested on his head. Although much shorter than Cornelius, this burly half-wit had huge forearms which had been responsible for more than its share of broken bones while training his men. Cornelius entered the training yard in a relatively clean tunic. He gazed over a dozen gladiators and cursed himself for being put into such a deplorable situation.

"Are you here to fight or pose?" Scaurius said, tossing a fist full of dirt at the new recruit.

Pointing to the man's dirty garment, Cornelius said, "You're a brave little fellow, but oblivious to intelligence. Have you no dignity of dress?"

The other gladiators stopped their maneuvers and watched in knowing anticipation.

"I don't know what you just said, but it sounded like an insult," Scaurius said, grabbing Cornelius' hand and bending it grotesquely.

Cornelius twisted around and jabbed his elbow squarely in the middle of the trainer's back. Scaurius backed off in pain, but quickly recouped, and dove at Cornelius' knees. This sent both of them to the ground, face up and in pain.

Stretching his hand to make his acquaintance, the short one said, "I'm your trainer, Scaurius. You must be Cornelius, the builder. You move well."

As they struggled to get to their feet, Tarontius Milo, well known for his fierce battles, lowered his hand to help Cornelius. After pulling him up halfway, he let him drop back to the ground. With a smirk to his fellow fighters, the big Greek strutted away, making his status as top fighter known to the newcomer.

"Save it for the games, Tarontius," Scaurius commanded as he rubbed his sore back.

The gladiator troupe's owner was an old senatorial member by the name of Sunius Amandus. He was pure business. He counted his money before and after each day of the games to ensure accuracy. He looked upon his gladiators not as humans but as profit levels based on skill. Injury or death meant nothing to him even though he preferred his better known fighters to keep winning. The more a veteran won, the less had to be spent on training him. In Cornelius, he saw a large man with potential to become one of his best money makers.

Cornelius was a quick study. His intelligence was unparalleled among the recruits. It didn't take him long to realize he had little choice but to train well. He would learn as much as he could and be aware of his surroundings at all times, or he would lose his life. He stayed by himself, not wanting to know the men who could one day be his opponents. His major distracter, Tarontius, was well known for his wins and used intimidation to his utmost advantage. His practice habits were every bit as exceptional as his fighting techniques. He kept a close eye on Cornelius while humiliating anyone who dared to spar with him. Scaurius thought it best not to allow Tarontius to tangle with Cornelius. He would bring his new and promising gladiator along at a good steady pace.

XII

AUC 832 (AD 79)

It was another hot day on August 21. Veturia's patience, waiting to marry Parosius was growing thin and the death of Vespasian would only delay his political career. She decided she could wait no longer to broach the subject with her father. Veturius was in his study conversing with a man when Veturia interrupted and asked her father to have the stranger step out for a moment.

"Father, I know how fond you are of Parosius," Veturia started.

"He is a fine man and will be a remarkable Aedile."

"Mother also finds him wonderful," she said meekly as her father looked up from his work.

"Sometimes, my daughter, it's best to push the knife directly into the heart than to pierce the surrounding areas. Sit and state your request."

Veturia sat as requested and dropped her head into her palms, with elbows resting on her father's desk. She then raised her head and confidently said, "I wish to marry Parosius."

Veturius looked back at his young daughter and paused in thought. Long standing tradition, his honor, his place on the senate floor, and finally his heritage, all stood like pillars between him and his beloved Veturia's wish. *But, the builder did save Crescentius' life, did he not.* In the end however, it was the blood. It always was the blood. How could he break the ancient patrician line that held the three percent of Rome's population so far above ninety-seven percent of plebeians? Patrician blood was to be worshipped and rewarded—plebeian, spilled and used for the good of Rome.

"It is not a decision that falls on you alone, Veturia. This is a family matter that clings to our ancestors like a baby to his mother's teats. You know what's expected."

"Am I to be treated like a prized calf? Parosius is a fine man. You said so yourself. He will soon have an honored title."

"Title is one thing, blood is another."

"Times have changed, Father. Must we hold to such ridiculous traditions?"

"I cannot answer you at this time. Go, Daughter…go and let me with my thoughts," he said angrily.

Veturia stepped back and dashed out of her father's presence. She cried, not for the decision left open by her father, but because she saw something in his eyes that scared her. She saw the look of a man who was held by his traditions and could not break free from them.

In protest, Veturia called her servant to pack her belongings and to ready the coach for a long stay in Herculaneum, away from her father. Before she left Rome, she would search for Parosius and tell him of her plans. She would reveal her discussion with her father to her mother and no one else. Veturia kept another secret, but this one would have to wait.

Veturius loved his daughter very much and might have leaned toward approving the marriage she most desperately wanted, but another factor was interfering. After Veturia ran out, he asked the strange man to return to his tablinum. His guest, Giton, sat grinning from ear-to-ear. Veturius pressed the stranger, "I still find it hard to believe a man like Parosius would adjust the books in his favor. What proof do you have?"

"Question him. Look at his books. If he lies, look at the laborer. See how princely he benefits them with your money."

Veturius dropped a few coins into Giton's hand and sent him on his way. He dropped his head and prayed to the goddess, Isis. Surely his prayers would be answered and what he had heard would be proven false. Veturius was a secret disciple of the Stoic philosophy. Although he kept his beliefs apart from his duties as a senator, he knew in his heart the philosophy that all men, even slaves, were citizens of the universe. The worshipers of Isis believed the story of her mate, Osiris. When Osiris was dismembered by the god of darkness, it was Isis who searched for his remains and consequently reassembled his body and resurrected him. Therefore, all thoughts of rebirth and life were attributed to Isis. Slaves were a part of life, and although he felt them to be equal, circumstances put them in the situation they were in. Fate was what it was, but that didn't mean all Romans were to treat them harshly. It would be one thing for Parosius to treat his working slaves well, but quite another to use his money frivolously and without consent.

Veturia was mounting her coach when she stopped and saw her mother standing in front of a mirror through her bedroom window. She told her aides to wait while she said farewell.

"Mother, I mean to leave this place. Father is being unreasonable."

"I did not bring you up to say harsh words against your father. Give it time, dear Veturia...he needs time to think it through," Livia said, unlocking her jewelry box. "This will be yours to wear on the day you wed—and you will wed," she said, holding an exquisitely large pearl earring in her hand.

"It is beautiful, Mother, but what good is one earring? Where is the other?"

"One earring is enough when it is this one. It is a special treasure. Sit down and I will tell you all about it."

"I've not the time. Tell Father his daughter went to Herculaneum. Perhaps my absence will unlock his stubborn mind."

"Maybe you're right, my daughter. I hope you are. Your father is a giving and wonderful man, but also very powerful. Don't push him too far."

"It is he who pushes too far, Mother," the headstrong Veturia vented. She then thought that perhaps a bit of caution was in order. "Maybe it would be best if you didn't tell father of my absence, at least not for a while."

"I will not be dishonest to your father."

"I'm not asking you to be dishonest, just slightly…ah…absent minded. Our disagreement would only grow if he sent a contingency to track me down and bring me back."

"Until nightfall—you have until then. Be careful on your journey, my little one." she said hugging Veturia and leaving the room in tears. Veturia could smell the sweet fragrance her mother left behind. She turned, still mad at her father, and grasped the earring her mother had left behind before running to her coach.

Parosius' day was full. The morning would be spent with his father working on the amphitheater. He then planned to meet with Veturia before leaving for Pompeii in an attempt to stop his brother's gladiatorial debut. Today's work entailed getting his men to set a foundation for a large unfinished arch near an entrance. The arch was in honor of Titus' sack of Jerusalem. Plans for the piece had started long before the death of Vespasian and Titus' subsequent promotion to Caesar. It would take a couple of years to complete. During a break, Parosius sought shade from the relentless sun. He sat inside the amphitheater's base column and wiped beads of sweat from his chest and neck. A flask filled with fresh water was pushed against his shoulder.

"I see my father's arch poses quite a chore on such a day as this, does it not, Parosius Tacitus?" Julia Flavia said, handing him a towel.

The fourteen year old daughter of Emperor Titus wore a long golden gown with an array of brightly colored sashes. Her fingers, wrists and neck were adorned with her favorite jewelry. Her hair was dyed a golden-red and she wore it down, curled in ringlets. A spotless coach remained a stone's throw away, and the driver stood by as ordered. She wore thick makeup, but she didn't need to, as her beauty was evident.

Taking a drink from the flask, Parosius lowered his head slightly and stammered, "I didn't hear you approach. I am honored by your presence."

"My grandfather spoke of you often. I can see why," she said with eyes that took in the entirety of Parosius. "I wanted to see the progress of my father's arch and to ask you if you...needed anything."

Parosius stood and looked down upon the new Emperor's daughter.

"I have everything I need. The arch will be a great testament to your father's deeds, though its finish is some time away," he said as diplomatically as he could.

Leaning in on tiptoes she pressed her lips to the side of Parosius' neck. "Are you sure you have everything you desire?"

Stunned and confused, he looked over Julia's head and saw Veturia peering at them from a distance. Their eyes met momentarily. Parosius could see her expression change to complete pain. Veturia turned away, leaving Rome without hesitation. Parosius' mind buzzed, searching for an answer. If he were to give in to Julia's passion, he could lose Veturia forever. If he ran after Veturia, leaving a fuming Julia behind, a word to her father could cost him his life. *What silky words would my brother spin in such a situation?*

Looking deep into young Julia's eyes, he said, "You are much too beautiful for someone like me. It hurts to even look upon you. Please go before it is too late. I could not bear to have you but only once…and once it would be should your father find out."

"But, Parosius…"

"It is for the best. I'll signal your coachman before we both regret it."

Parosius walked away with a satisfied smile. As soon as Julia was out of sight, he ran for Veturia. Not finding her, he rode his steed to her father's villa where her mother ran to him and revealed Veturia's plan. Parosius gathered his friend Publius and with their work coach, immediately set out after Veturia, riding swiftly down the Via Appia.

They caught up with her on their second day of riding, when a tired Publius spotted a partially closed coach carrying a rider and three aides. As they approached, the earth below them rumbled, causing them to fall from their horses. When the tremor subsided, Veturia jumped from her coach and ran to Parosius.

"Are you hurt? What was that? Can you move?" she said in a nervous voice, kissing him all over his face. Parosius opened his eyes sluggishly. He glanced over at Publius sprawled on the ground and winked at him. Dropping him harshly to the ground Veturia said, "You're not hurt at all, and I'm not talking to you." She got up and marched to her coach.

"What about me?" Publius pleaded.

Veturia's response was a look that would have silenced a charging bull.

"You don't understand. It was Titus' daughter. I was cornered."

"Big, bad Julia forced her way on you, did she? You can lift a stone pillar, but can't fight off a small girl?"

"Nothing happened then, just as nothing would happen with any one else, but you."

Turning back to Parosius, she asked with a smile that came from deep within, "Will you escort me to Herculaneum so we can properly make this incident disappear?"

"Only until Sinuessa, from there I must attend to my brother in Pompeii. I promise to meet you in a few days." From his wrist he removed a solid gold bracelet, inside of which was clearly etched with the name *Tacitus*. "Please take and keep this. It has been in our family for as long as anyone can remember."

Veturia took the bracelet and pushed it all the way up her arm, where the heavy keepsake rested loosely on her bicep. With misty eyes, she removed a ring from her finger. "This is to be put in a special place and given to my daughter when the time comes. It is yours until that day." Parosius inserted a length of twine through the ring and, after tying the ends, slipped it over his head, letting the ring rest on his chest.

The earth moved several more times as they rode along. The longer they traveled, the more the horses and the cattle along the road grew excited, shuffling in an odd way. Birds were becoming strangely scarce. Villagers were moving to what they believed to be safer ground, many of them still recalling the destruction that befell them seventeen years earlier. Below them stress was building up between two huge drifting block's of the earth's crust. During the last quake, the earth trembled violently—especially near Pompeii. "As many as six hundred sheep were swallowed in a single gulp," said one Roman who wasted no time in temporarily moving his family this time around. The destruction, although not complete, had been massive. Now, those that remember prayed that it not happen again. Of late, the countryside of Vesuvius had seen odd changes—wells were drying up, and springs ceased to flow.

Reaching Sinuessa, Parosius embraced Veturia and bid her farewell.

The calm green pastures of Vesuvius hulked over their left shoulder as they went their separate ways. Herculaneum and Pompeii were only ten miles apart. Baring any setbacks with his brother, Parosius felt sure he would be back in the arms of Veturia within a couple of days.

Abruptly, the earth moved and twisted. Parosius looked back at Veturia, now hundreds of yards away. Dust was moving with the wind as the ground cracked and opened in jagged turns. The smell of sulfur and the feeling of heat entered their senses. The coach that held Veturia and her three aides dipped dangerously into a newly formed opening within the earth. The strain broke the ties to their team of horses sending the coach deeper into an opening, but freeing their horses. Parosius, his eyes wide with terror, turned around and commanded his horse to sprint toward Veturia. Both horse and rider moved deftly, dodging each new fracture. Publius rode madly behind him like a shadow. Parosius reached the coach as it sank further into the earth, held awkwardly aloft by moving clay and rock. A slave stretched his arm down to Veturia who scrambled out from the front seat. Their arms locked, but both began to slide into the depths. Parosius reached desperately and grasped the slave, and in-turn Veturia, while the ground moved violently once more. The coach moved hard to one side entangling Veturia's leg around the broken horse straps. Parosius swung his sword down at the straps and freed her from the coach. Publius gathered the coach's frightened horses and tied a rope to their harness while throwing the other end to Parosius. Publius directed the team to pull, while Parosius held on and dragged both the slave and Veturia out of the steaming cavity. Veturia pleaded for the lives of her other two aides as they struggled in the back of the coach. Parosius madly tried to tie the rope to the front of the coach, but it began to sink farther into the earth. The coach jerked and turned and finally dropped out of sight.

Looking down into the hole, Veturia cried, "They were with me all of my life." Parosius, holding her tight, picked her up and carried her away from the open depths.

VESUVIUS

Parosius offered their coach to Veturia and her remaining slave. He had almost lost his love and did not want to leave, but as the rumbling subsided he knew he had to try and help his brother before returning to Herculaneum and Veturia. Parosius and Publius would ride bareback to Pompeii.

XIII

On August 23, Pompeii was bustling. The sun hid behind clouds as revelers walked briskly down dusty roads hurrying to the amphitheater and the games. Excitement was in the air for the anticipation of Vulcanalia—festival of the Roman god of fire. The popularity of the events was extremely high, especially during such a celebratory day as this. Entrance was free for any Roman citizen. The women were directed to the top tier while the men occupied all other seating. The morning activities began with slaves, and those that refused to worship the gods of the Emperor, such as Christians. Those were first to die in the games as they were pitted against a variety of wild animals. The smell of fresh blood was in the air. On this day the stench of sulfur was also in the mix as the earth rumbled just enough to let the residence know that something wasn't quite right. Lions, mad dogs, and tigers were among the hungry beasts that gave the spectators a taste of what was to come. Before the carnage began, the animals had been teased with the taste of human flesh to teach them whom they needed to attack. The beast-master felt good about his animals. But his job was not without risk. Should any of them turn away and refuse to attack, the events host could order the beast-master to be pushed into the arena and put to death by sword. On this day at least, he was spared—unlike the victims of his beasts.

By mid-morning the public executions began. Heads rolled to a count of two dozen sentenced criminals. Before each decapitation, the convict's crime and sentence was read out loud. As they were dragged to the podium, the more they fought, the louder the crowd cheered.

When Parosius and Publius arrived in Pompeii to plead for the release of Cornelius, the magistrates of Pompeii would have none of it. Cornelius was to fight in the afternoon. To make matters worse, his opponent was to be Pompeii's favorite, Tarontius. The magistrate, Stuvius, left nothing to chance in his vengeance to see Cornelius pay for his indiscretions with his wife.

Several fights would wet the spectators' appetite before the main attraction between the Greek murderer, Tarontius, and the adulterer, Cornelius. Many early matches were fought as two-on-two battles. One such battle pitted four gladiatrices. The Ethiopians wore long arm guards, holding curved shields with the left and a gladius in the right. The combatants wore precious little to cover their breast. The ploy to excite the largely male audience did just that. The crowd cheered at a high pitch until two combatants laid their helmets to the ground, admitting defeat. The main event was about to begin.

The arena was cleared when a short, balding man stood from a podium and ceremoniously announced the final and featured fight of the day. Both gladiators entered the arena from opposite sides. Between them, and up on the first tier, was the stage for the elite. Honored with the center chair sat Decimus Stuvius. Below them on ground level, but behind metal bars, Parosius and Publius looked on in frustrated helplessness. Flanked by several amphitheater guards, Parosius called out encouragement to his brother.

"Use your brain as well as your brawn, my brother," Parosius shouted.

"I only hope my brain is a fast as his brawn," Cornelius yelled back as he revealed his chosen weapons, two gladi—short swords. His chest was bare, with just enough clothing to cover the essentials below the waist. His only protection was a light open helmet. Tarontius approached fully armored. He wore a helmet crested with a stylized griffin, leg wrappings, and shin-guards. Carrying a gladius and a small, round shield, he approached Cornelius with the confidence of immortality. Cornelius immediately began to use his speed and quickness to attack the protected Tarontius. After a slashing move by the Greek's sword, Cornelius ducked. He then twirled down and around the back of his opponent, tearing at his thigh with his weapon. Tarontius wheeled back at the same time and caught the side of Cornelius' head with his shield, delivering a bone-jarring blow. Cornelius sailed onto the dusty ground as Tarontius glanced at his leg wound. The Pompeians cheered wildly for the well known gladiator. Cornelius shook his head both from the blast of Tarontius and to block out the negative banter from the crowd. Approaching with renewed respect, the two circled each other looking for a weakness. Cornelius lunged and scraped Tarontius' left shoulder. Leaving himself momentarily open, Cornelius received another swift jolt from the shield of Tarontius. Sprawling to the ground, Cornelius struggled to get up, while the muscular, but bloodied Tarontius closed in. While on one knee, Cornelius blocked several stabbing attempts, but received a glancing rip to the forearm. Still dazed and now dripping with sweat and blood, he somehow found the strength to stand. Retreating, the spectators began to sense another win for their hero. Hearing the cheers, Tarontius raised his sword and shield to the sky, inciting the people as he whirled in circles. Backing at least twenty-five steps away from his foe, Cornelius turned his gladius blade-side to his hand.

He reached back and unleashed his weapon through the air. The gladius hit Tarontius in the right shoulder, slicing clear through to the back. Tarontius screamed in a low and garbled tone, dropping his sword. Now bleeding from three distinct areas of his massive body, he reached and grimaced painfully, pulling mightily on the handle of Cornelius' gladius. He removed it, pushed the blade into the ground, and broke it with the heel of his boot. His right arm now useless, he threw his shield to the ground and picked up his sword. The spectators let out a loud cheer for their hurting hero.

Both warriors faced each other in the middle of the arena. Cornelius was clearly at an advantage. Tarontius' breath was heavy, and the crowd's cheering began to fade. Tarontius made one last attempt and pushed his weapon at Cornelius' neck. Cornelius dodged the blade, and with Tarontius' arm stretched out, he brought his gladius down on the big man's fist, clipping off several fingers. Tarontius stood blood-soaked and weaponless. He dropped to his knees and awaited his fate. Cornelius raised his gladius to the podium awaiting the magistrate's signal on the life or death of the loser. The spectators presented themselves as a fickle sort. Moments ago they had worshipped the gladiator, Tarontius. Now a slight majority wanted him dead. Stuvius, not known for his compassion, surprised everyone when he raised his hand with thumb inside his fist granting life to the fallen gladiator.

Parosius and Publius hugged each other in relief at Cornelius' victory. As Tarontius was removed from the arena, the Pompeians jeered in infuriation. *How could their hero be bested by this Roman womanizer?* Their anger seemed to be building. Stuvius decided not to disappoint his people. With a nod of his head, a wild tiger was released. It was huge and spotted Cornelius right off. The scent of his blood made the beast's target an easy one. As Cornelius approached the eastern exit gates, they were abruptly closed. Several columns down, Parosius saw the beast crouch from behind ready to spring on his brother. The spectators were now cheering loudly and Cornelius could not hear his brother's warnings. Without hesitation, Parosius hit a guard squarely on the jaw. Publius retrieved the keys from the fallen soldier and opened the gates before them. Parosius ran to the beast and with his sword in hand he pierced it through the heart as it jumped at him. Cornelius turned to see the downed beast as his brother was quickly surrounded by a host of guards. Publius ran to help his friends, but they were clearly outmanned. Parosius managed to reach Publius and said, "Find my sword and bring it to Veturia. She'll know what to do."

Finding it on the ground among all the guards and now the crowd, he snatched it and ran from arena. Running through the town he found his horse and headed for Herculaneum.

XIV

Both Parosius and Cornelius were marched south through the streets until they reached an old prison. Many of those they passed recognized them from the amphitheater and applauded them as celebrities. This they found strange under the circumstances. They were pushed past a set of guards, and down a dirt road to a long row of prison cells—the same cells they had hoped not to enter during Cornelius' hearing. A door was opened, and they were tossed into a dark pit smelling of wood, earth, and excrement. A small window with wooden bars was built into the heavy door and would be their only source of light. The cell base was several feet below the bottom of the door.

"Perhaps if we increased our rent," Cornelius joked as he attempted to stand.

Suddenly a cold plate of porridge sailed through the opening.

"The service seems a bit rushed. I'll need to have a talk with the cook," Parosius said.

They laughed together, as brothers do. Then they stopped. The silence brought realization. They were likely to be left here until their death sentence. They both hoped Publius made his way out of Pompeii. He may be their only hope. No one, other than the Pompeian elite knew where they were, not even Publius.

Parosius punched the muddy wall violently. "They will pay for this. Publius will see to it."

"He's a good friend and has a sharp wit. I have no doubt he'll do what he can," Cornelius said as his brother ripped pieces of cloth from his tunic and applied it to his wounds.

Now both sat with their knees up and arms crossed over their shins. "Thank you, Brother," Cornelius said, breaking the silence.

"For what?"

"For saving my life!"

Parosius looked at their surroundings. "It appears as though I may have only prolonged it."

"Just the same, I thank you."

After a long reflective pause, Parosius ventured, "What of your trainer and your troupe owner? Would they not gain money by renting out the gladiator who defeated Tarontius?"

"That is a thought, but based on Stuvius' eagerness to see me dead, I'm sure my owner will be taken care of handsomely to hand me over."

"The sun begins to go down. Let's rest and find answers tomorrow."

The cries were not simultaneous, but periodic and filled with fright. The unexpected shrieks shocked the prisoners to their feet. It was just before midnight on the 23rd of August. A light powdering of ash began to enter the small opening on their door. Parosius jumped up as far as he could and grabbed the wooden bar. He pulled himself up and looked out. People were running from the roads, looking for cover. Lightning was striking everywhere, and a steady rain was falling. A guard stood under a lantern that hung from the overhang of a tiled roof across the road. Parosius called out to him.

"Guard, what's happening? Why are the people running?"

"It is nothing. They say the mountain is coughing angrily. It'll quiet down by morning. Go to sleep and quit bothering me or I'll make sure your cell is missed for feeding tomorrow."

"You promise?"

Parosius let go of the bar and collapsed on the ground. The two slept from pure exhaustion despite their circumstances and the occasional cries heard from outside. As the early morning came and went, the cloud cover kept the day's light hazy. From their small opening they could still see ashes falling to the ground.

It wasn't until early afternoon that they were startled to their feet by a colossal crack. The plug that had long sealed the throat of Vesuvius' opened at the crater floor under tremendous pressure. Fragmented molten rock shot high into the sky and formed a mushroom cloud, as the particles broke apart into smaller, deadly pieces. The winds blew hard to the southwest as Pompeii and Stabiae began to feel the wrath of Vesuvius.

"Let us out!" the voices shouted from the line of cells. People were running in every direction. Many Pompeians had left their homes days ago, frightened from tremors—those that remained now wished they had gone with them. Cornelius, still weak from his match at the arena, sat while Parosius jumped to grasp the opening. He could see the people running for cover under the roof across the road. Some were being killed by rock that hurled down on them. The pumice was light and porous, but no less dangerous as they sailed down at incredible speeds.

Parosius dropped to the ground. "Maybe we're safer in here."

The screams would not stop. Death and destruction continued all around them. Hours passed and Vesuvius continued to spew its rock into the sky. Parosius looked out once again and saw the debris rising from the ground, higher and higher.

"I don't think we can stay here, Cornelius."

"Do we have a choice?"

Parosius ordered his brother to get down on all fours. Standing on Cornelius' back, he then pounded on the door's wooden bars. His fist became bloodied and near broken, but he was able to dislodge a couple of them. Visibility was getting difficult as the cloud of debris now totally covered the sun. People were still running in terror. As one young man ran by, Parosius reached out and caught the frightened teenager around the neck.

"Unlatch the door and I'll let you keep your head. It's down near your waist. That's it! Just lift it!" Parosius ordered.

Parosius let go of the lad and pushed on the door. The debris wedged the door shut, and it took both Parosius and Cornelius to move it just enough to squeeze through. The brothers held their positions just outside their cell and took in what they couldn't see from within. Standing upon a foot of pumice and stone, they witnessed roofs caving in, women and children being pummeled, and fires everywhere as oil spilled from street lamps. Rather than flee, some of the Roman prison guards felt allegiance and remained behind. Parosius and Cornelius saw one coming their way. They turned around the corner and leaned up against the prison wall. Parosius took the twine from around his neck, removed the ring Veturia had given him, and put it on his baby finger—only up to the first knuckle—

135

it could go no further. As the guard walked by, he pulled the twine over the guard's head, dropped it around his neck, and pulled hard until the man stopped breathing. Returning the ring to the bloodied twine, he again placed it upon his chest.

Making sure to stay under the lip of the tiled roof, they ran down the stretch of prison cells and freed the remaining prisoners. Together they charged the rest of the guards, took their metal shields, and held them over their heads to ward off pumice stones and rock. They then joined the masses that ran through the streets. The passages were rampant with slaves, freedmen, criminals—the poor as well as the rich. On this day, all men were indeed equal. As they ran, the screams of pain intensified. Roofs made of weak wood collapsed onto all those that had hoped they were protected. Thirst now became a problem, as the pumas and ash sucked much of the moisture from the air.

They ran to the stable that housed the horses of Parosius and Publius. Cornelius quickly took a sheath, sword, and pack of food from Publius' horse. Parosius took only his special wine cup and tethered it to his belt. The horses would be worthless to them in all the debris.

"We need a plan or we'll not see tomorrow, Brother," Cornelius said.

All of Pompeii was surrounded by an enclosed wall. The wall was 30 feet high in many places. One hundred and sixty acres of sloping earth included many gates that allowed entrance and departure to each specific region. A tall tower stood by each gate and soldiers were stationed there to perform their task of opening the gate every morning and closing it every night. As Parosius and Cornelius set out to the Marina Gate they noticed it was open and there were no soldiers to be seen. There breathing became more and more laborious with each step. Still they made it to a long, steep stairway and ramp that led to the Sarno River. Far below, and between lightning strikes, they could see many boats along the river bed—most were buried under the falling debris.

Parosius eyed the area and began to devise a plan. If they could make it safely to a boat, they might set out and paddle down the river to the Bay of Neapolis. From there, with luck, he could make it to the beaches of Herculaneum and find his beloved Veturia.

"It won't work. You'll be killed," Cornelius said, reading his brother's mind.

"What do you mean, I'll be killed? We'll be killed."

"You know I can't go with you. I don't mix well with water."

"The sky is breaking apart and you're worried about the water?" an incredulous Parosius asked.

"I'll help you, my brother, but I'm not going with you."

Most of what was coming down now was the size of pebbles and reached as high as their knees. Their leather boots would likely make the trip, but their bodies could not take too many more hits. Their skin was bruised and burned, but it was now or never. From under the tower, they sprinted toward the boats with shields over their heads. Parosius ran for a small skiff that was partially submerged in water, due to the weight of the pumice. Cornelius helped him empty the vessel. It was built for two and typically used for fishing. As Parosius was about to board, several other terrified Pompeians attempted to seize it. Cornelius pushed his brother into the boat. While others fought to get in, Parosius picked up an oar and beat them back. Though pumice floated on the water like a dark blanket, the current took him down-stream quickly. He shouted to Cornelius, but the distance was too great to be heard. Cornelius ran back to the Marina Gate and turned just long enough to see his brother heading towards the bay.

Veturia arrived in Herculaneum about mid-day on the 23rd of August. Through the next twenty-four hours, Vesuvius kept the locals on alert. Most of the people that called the seaport their home did not sit idle. They felt the blast and saw the cloud over the big mountain. Although their homes, apartments, and shops did not yet feel the wrath of the volcano, many decided it was best to move temporarily from the danger. Veturia passed many who were going in the opposite direction. The sky was dim and lightening shot out everywhere. Much to the disapproval of her two remaining servants, Alecius and Diatrus, the stubborn Veturia resolved to wait for Parosius at her father's villa, as planned.

Veturia did not attempt to sleep. She ordered Alecius to pack supplies, should they need to make a quick exit. As pumice and rock began to fall, she ran about the villa securing her family's belongings. Then, kneeling before the statue of Isis, she prayed for the goddess to hear her and give her mercy. Her servant Alecius continued to plead with her to leave, but Veturia resisted. It was then that a dirty, tired visitor approached them. Veturia barely recognized, Publius.

"Veturia, you're still here. I thought you would have left for safer ground," Publius said in a quick garbled voice.

Veturia looked beyond Publius but did not see what she was looking for. "Publius, please sit, you look terrible. Diatrus, fetch him some wine. I'm afraid our water dried up some time ago."

"I've been better," he said as he sat struggling to get a good breath of air. After a long drink he walked out to his stolen horse and returned. "I have something for you."

Veturia recognized the sword right off. She knew Parosius would never part with it.

With her head down she asked, "What has happened to Parosius."

"He's alive, Veturia. He's been arrested. Things did not go well in Pompeii. He tried to help his brother and the locals didn't take kind to such interference. He said if you saw the sword you would know what to do."

"My father and I are not seeing eye-to-eye these days. But he does think much of Parosius. He will demand Parosius be released."

"I'm afraid we have other problems to concern ourselves with first," Publius said as the ground shook once more. He walked outside and could hear faint screams with a certain madness coming from Herculaneum.

"We'll rest for a short while, but if it gets much worse out there we will need to leave to find safe ground. You won't be able to help Parosius if you're dead, Veturia."

They talked of Parosius and his troubles in Pompeii and then Publius drifted off to a much needed sleep. Veturia cleaned her lover's sword and placed it in a keyed box used to conceal family valuables. She then dictated a letter to Diatrus and instructed her to leave for

Rome immediately. Veturia could not sleep and as the air became dry and difficult to take in, she woke her friend.

She pushed on the shoulder of her sleeping friend. With the great mountain only miles away Herculaneum's citizens became increasingly frightened.

"Publius, many are taking to the beach. With Parosius held in Pompeii, I see no point in staying here. Perhaps we should leave."

Until now, Vesuvius had been killing by the sheer direction of the wind. Herculaneum did not have the downpour of pumice that Pompeii was experiencing, but in the very early morning of August 25th, it chose another way to display its awesome power. The enormous column that was an immovable circular wall, spewing from within, was about to collapse. Glowing matter waited to shoot down the sides of the mountain as if in a race to the finish line. The avalanche was about to roll in two distinct waves; a fast-moving swarm of ash and gases, followed by a dense flow of pumice, rock fragments, and soil. All was made fluid by the extreme heat. Five times hotter than boiling water, it would travel at nearly one hundred miles per hour. The deadly combination pointed itself toward Herculaneum.

On the beach were a host of boat chambers. A multitude of Herculaneum citizens were scrambling to get any boats that remained in the chambers out to the sea. Publius, Veturia and Alecius ran to the northern most chamber. They stood in front of it with others who were waiting to board a boat—any boat. One such boat arrived from the sea. A man jumped out, while several others poured in. That man was Parosius. Many from inside the boat chamber began to run toward the boat as well, when suddenly the Bay of Neapolis pushed itself temporarily onto the land as if breathing out. Just as quickly the water receded. Seconds later a wave of ash and gases ran through Herculaneum and approached the beach. Parosius, who was pushed about by the bays fickle water, got to his feet and scanned the horrified people inside the boat chambers. Through the darkened sky and the smoke filled air he finally saw his Veturia and ran towards her. He reached out to the one woman he would have given anything for. Veturia cried as she saw Parosius drop to his knees and collapse from the gases. Publius held her back, but only for a moment, as hot ashes choked the life out of all of them. Veturia died, there, at that moment only a boat-length away from her beloved Parosius. She lay still, unable to feel his touch one more time—unable to tell him of his child that grew inside her.

XV

Most of the lives of Herculaneum were quickly extirpated after the first wave. Some died at the homes they refused to leave. There were prisoners who were confined and could not leave, drunks who didn't know any better, and thieves who found this the perfect time to purloin valuables. Dozens were mowed down on the beach and hundreds in the boat chambers. The intense heat made all soft tissue disappear and brains evaporate inside their heads. It was like swallowing fire, but only for a second.

Over and over Vesuvius expelled an ash cloud and followed each with a wave of molten rock. Layers of each wave formed hideously over the doomed seaport. The sixth eruption was its last. Ash continued to blanket the area for several days. The shoreline was extended several hundred yards into the Bay of Neapolis. When the sky finally opened and the sun shed light on the destruction, those that escaped began to return. They mourned the lost lives of those they loved and slowly tried to understand the inevitable and permanent loss of their possessions.

Pliny the Elder died on the shore of Stabiae, overcome by fumes. His nephew, Pliny the Younger wrote a detailed account of the day's events and gathered information on many of the people involved with the disaster.

Cornelius Tacitus made it out of harm's way and eventually back to Rome. With his accuser Decimus Stuvius a victim of Vesuvius, he was granted another hearing in Rome. None other than the portly man himself, Quintus, won him his freedom during an eloquent, but lengthy speech on the "tainted and error filled" trial he had received from the biased Pompeians. The senate members were only too happy to set Cornelius free, if only to get Quintus to stop talking. Cornelius immediately returned to his work on the amphitheater with his father, Lucius. He was instrumental with the inclusion of his brother Parosius' likeness, which was added to the south arch entrance. Below the massive carving were the words "Parosius Tacitus, constructum ab Flavian Amphitheater" or "Parosius Tacitus, builder of the Flavian Amphitheater". If not for his persistence and the monetary backing of Veturius Fortunatus, the monument would never have been approved. Cornelius Tacitus was granted the equestrian order and went on to become a famous historian, who lived well into his eighties. His father, Lucius, also enjoyed a long life.

Veturia's mother, Livia, did not live to see the winter. Her imagined illnesses soon became real and her heart stopped on her 34th birthday.

Her husband and Veturia's father, Veturius Fortunatus was never quite the same. He spent much of his last years wandering the blackened ruins above where he believed Herculaneum to be buried. It was not the loss of his exquisite villa that he mourned, but that of his precious daughter. Deep within himself he may have known the futility of his search, but outwardly he could not be convinced of the loss. When finally and thankfully he was in death's grip, his request was to have his servants mix his remains with the ashes of his late wife. They then were to spread them over the encased port of Herculaneum. He requested that they pray to the goddess Isis, beseeching her to allow their earthly dust to seep closer to his Veturia during each rain—until he could surround her body and comfort it, gather it, and resurrect it.

Crescentius, son of Veturius Fortunatus, did not squander his father's inheritance. His businesses included the building of many great Roman monuments.

The Emperor Titus did not have luck on his side. A natural leader, he could have turned out to be as great an Emperor as his father, had it not been for happenstance. His defeat of the Jews in a long and victorious military career made him a favorite, but Vesuvius took much from him. Then there were the devastating fires one year later, and finally a rebellion led by Terentius Maximus. If not for the glorious inaugural of the Flavian Amphitheater he might have fallen out of favor and lost his role as emperor as well as his life. As it was, the Amphitheater helped to keep Titus hugely popular. Just as things were beginning to take hold for him, he became ill. Only two years after his father died, he succumbed to fever. A persistent rumor holds that his brother Domitian may have poisoned him.

Titus' young brother, Domitian became Emperor upon his death and held the position for fifteen years. Domitian did not have the military background of his father and brother. His personality was known to be cruel. At one point he developed a passion for his niece, Julia Flavia, daughter of Titus, kidnapping her while dismissing Julia's husband. Julia died in AD 91 during an abortion. Domitian was murdered in September of AD 96, in a plot by senatorial enemies, one of whom was Stephanus, the steward of the deceased Julia Flavia.

16

Present Day Herculaneum

As the large Roman's remains were being cleaned and moved, Professor Stowald saw a flicker of gold resting in a rock near his chest area. He bent down and carefully removed a gold ring. After rinsing the artifact in solution, he handed it to Oliver. Looking through his reading glasses, he had hoped to find markings, a name, anything that might indicate it had belonged to Parosius or Veturia. He found nothing. Minutes later Doctor Ballantonio handed a large gold bracelet to Cassandra. It had been found near Veturia's remains. Resting it on her palm, she examined it in the hot sun. Turning it up to look on the inside, she saw it. Marked large, and with little damage, was the name, *Parosius Tacitus.*

Cassandra looked up and cried, "It's her, Grandpa. It's Veturia Fortunatus. She had Parosius' bracelet." She sat on a rounded bolder and began to sob. "They couldn't reach each other. It's not fair."

Mee knelt down next to the Roman woman with her arm reaching out and then gazed at the remains of the large man on the beach. She stood and uncharacteristically wiped a tear from her eye.

Oliver now understood why he was meant to be here, at this time in his life. He understood why, in 1982, his trip to Herculaneum wasn't meant to be. And finally he understood why he'd been having those recurring dreams. His grandfather, Demetri, wanted him to finish the story. The story began with two young Romans who were separated in life by the mighty force of Vesuvius. Oliver's task was to put the pieces back together. He now understood the why, but had yet to realize how solving one mystery can lead to so many others.

Dr. Ballantonio fit the jewelry back where they found it and began snapping pictures and making notes. Except for the continual removal of volcanic debris, everything was to be left as it was over nineteen hundred years earlier. Oliver and Cassandra determined that they needed more time and called their tour manager to leave without them. They would attempt to catch up with the tour on their return trip from Sorrento. Mee and Luke thanked everyone for their kindness and left, saying they wanted to continue with the tour.

Cassandra handed Professor Stowald the box of Isis and watched as he looked intently over the ancient letters. With one raised eyebrow he said, "We must do more research, but this is very, very intriguing."

"They were meant to be together, Grandpa." Cassandra said as they sat in their hotel room that night.

Oliver walked out on the balcony and looked at the bright stars. "You're right, of course. But we're not even positive that it *is* them. Sandro…that is Dr. Ballantonio said he was going to do some more research to see if he can find any more clues about their identity. Let's wait and see what he comes up with." Oliver studied his granddaughter's eyes. "If you're thinking what I think you're thinking, you better stop. I have to confess, I'm not sure that this trip to Italy will be my last. If you tamper at all with who we believe to be Parosius and Veturia and you're caught, we would never be welcomed back here."

Just then Cassandra's phone rang. "Cassandra, it's Mee. Could you get to the lab? It's about your Roman lovers."

"What do you mean? What's going on?"

"Just get over here, right away." Those were the last words Cassandra heard before hearing the click of the phone.

Putting on her shoes, Cassandra said with a wink, "I'll be back, Grandpa. Don't wait up."

"Who was that?"

"Ah, it was Dr. Ballantonio. He wants to go out for a drink and talk about bones. You know doctors."

"Have a good time. I have my books and my laptop. I'll be fine. Be careful. Don't do anything stupid."

"When have you ever known me to...oh never mind. Good night!"

Fifteen minutes later, Cassandra's little lie became real. The doctor was unlocking the lab door.

"Mee called...What's wrong?...Are you okay? She said you were here and needed help," Sandro Ballantonio asked.

Cassandra thought for a while and smiled to herself, thinking this was Mee's way to get her and Sandro together.

"I'm fine," she said looking at the handsome Italian. "I think Mee was playing a little game, but as long as we're here, I do have a question."

"Say no more, you wish for me to show you...what you call...night-life...fun? Come, we drive to Sorrento and taste the wine."

"That sounds like fun, but sadly, Doctor Ballantonio, that isn't what's on my mind. Ordinarily I would never ask you to do something to jeopardize your career, but ...."

Now raising Cassandra's hand and kissing it, "You need only ask. And please, call me Sandro."

Cassandra wetted her lips and looked deep into Sandro's eyes. Did she really like Sandro or was she pouring the charm on to get what she wanted? She thought maybe a little of both. "I would like to make an adjustment to what was discovered today out at the boat chambers and I'm asking for your help. Would you help me, Sandro?"

Sandro slowly released her hand and backed up a bit. "What sort of... adjustment?"

"I would like to move the remains of Parosius Tacitus so he can be with his lover Veturia. I would like to change your records to reflect such a thing."

"What of Dr. Stowald? He would not stand for this. I could go to jail for such a thing." Now turning away, "You ask too much."

Cassandra's mind was racing. *Quit and go back to the hotel or keep trying—and what of Sandro's job? Is my obsession worth the risk?* Earlier in the day she knew what she had to do and now she was beginning to lose her focus. No, this had to be done. "With or without you, Sandro, they must be reunited." She turned her head and tears started to fall. Not tears used as a devise to lure Sandro's help, but real ones.

"You are sure this is what you want? I still have more research to prove they are who you say they are," Sandro said as his defenses were melting away.

"Will you help me, Sandro?"

With a nod of his head, "Who can argue if you do something out of love?"

"Sandro, what about the security guards? Won't they wonder what we're doing? Won't they stop us?"

Sandro raised his hand to cover the smirk on his face. "To tell the truth, they pretty much sleep through the night. I've come here many nights to check on things and they don't even move."

Sandro went to a locker and retrieved two brown overalls and a stretcher with a thin metal bottom, used to carry whole skeletons without disrupting the bone structure. With flashlights turned off, they quietly walked down to the beach site. The stars were plentiful and the moon was only a sliver as they approached the chamber. The excavators had dug completely around and under the remains of Parosius and Veturia during the day. The move would not be as difficult as Sandro had thought. He reached down and carefully slid the metal sheet under the large Roman. Suddenly they were blinded by the brightness of spot lights. Two Italian guards, hired for night duty to protect the chambers, pointed their weapons on the frightened intruders. Sandro and Cassandra held up their arms and turned in their direction.

"Dottore Ballantonio, perchè siete qui?" the guard asked the doctor.

Sandro addressed the guard as Alfonso. Though Cassandra could understand little of what they said, she could see that Sandro's answer seemed to pacify the guard.

The security guards thought of placing them in a holding room. As they pondered the situation, Alfonso received a call on his cell phone. After ending the call, he told his captives to go on their way and that Dr. Stowald would be talking to them in the morning. Cassandra and Sandro left, relieved for not being arrested, but glum for not being able to do as they had intended.

"They didn't appear to be asleep, Sandro!" Cassandra said with sarcasm. "What did you say to him?"

"They are uneasy tonight. He asked me what we were doing here." Sandro leaned against the laboratory wall and grinned. "I told him I was showing off in front of the pretty American girl and wanted to impress her with our find today. He asked me about the metal sheet and I told him I brought it so you wouldn't have to sit on the dirt."

Cassandra liked how he handled the confrontation, especially the part about being pretty. They went back to the lab and removed their overalls. The lone light was an exit sign above the far door. Cassandra felt defeated yet happy that Sandro believed in her enough to try. He had behaved like a friend telling you there's a "kick me" sign on your back before walking into class. You feel stupid and hurt about someone pulling a trick like that on you, but relieved you had a friend who didn't want you to be humiliated. Getting her foot caught as she tried to slide the garment over her tennis shoes, Cassandra lost her balance and fell into the strong arms of Sandro. They looked closely into each other's eyes and then kissed, long and softly.

"I sure could use some of that wine you were talking about earlier," Cassandra said as Sandro pulled her up.

Still holding her he said, "Then, wine you shall have."

Sandro drove her to a small pub not far from Herculaneum.

"I will make a toast," Sandro said lifting a glass. "To Parosius and Veturia, may they one day be united in death as they were in life."

Cassandra tapped her glass onto Sandro's and they continued lifting their glasses until the early morning.

Cassandra woke to rapid knocking on her hotel door. She had only been in bed for a couple of hours. Her head was pounding at the rhythm of the determined racket in the hall. Oliver rose, rested and ready to start a new day, despite the rude awakening. Given just enough time to dress, they were hastily escorted to the boat chamber site by the Italian police. Cassandra's face wore a guilty, tired look that matched Sandro's, who arrived from his Ercolano apartment in much the same fashion. Oliver stood by, surprisingly calm and collected.

Standing in front of chamber thirteen, Professor Stowald began, "Our guards were attacked last night around the time that both of you were here. Knocked unconscious, they woke to find our chest of artifacts in the chamber was missing. If it weren't for Oliver, you would both be behind bars as we speak. As it is, the officer will need to take you both in for questioning."

"I don't understand, Grandpa?"

"After you left last night, I did a little checking on our two friends from the tour bus. I may be old, but I can search my way around the internet with the best of them. I didn't trust them and I didn't like the way they were snooping around. Stowald was pretty accommodating with them yesterday. A few more minutes, and he might have given them a set of keys to the lab," Oliver said winking at his old buddy.

"I like inquisitive people," Stowald said.

"The first thing I checked was the roster for all planes that landed in Rome that day. The name 'Mee Lee' was not among them. Then I did a criminal background check on her and found that she was on probation for a few years back in San Francisco due to theft charges. Luke Trettin was a little harder. He had several different names. I called the San Francisco Police Department, and they said he was wanted for theft of museum paintings.

Dr. Stowald injected, "Oliver called me about 1:00 AM and asked that I keep special watch on things at the chambers. He explained why he was concerned, and I immediately called Alfonso. That's when Alfonso told me about intruders. He told me that Sandro was here with a young lady." Sandro stood with his arm around Cassandra. Dr. Stowald glanced at the two. "Until now I didn't realize it was Cassandra. A few hours later Alfonso called me back and said he, and the rest, had been knocked out. When they came to, the chest of artifacts was gone. One of the guards briefly saw their image in the darkness. His description matched the size of Mee Lee and Luke Trettin, but in the dark it could have just as well been the two of you. Near the area where the chest had been, we found this small hand-mirror. The mirror was in a plastic bag."

Cassandra stepped forward to look at it. "That... that's my mirror... how?"

"We also found blood on a pair of brown overalls, like those Alfonso said you were both wearing last night. When the blood is analyzed, it is believed that the blood will be that of our security guards.

"There are hair fibers to be analyzed as well," an officer from the Carabinieri police force said, with a thick Italian accent.

"Let me introduce Captain Claudio Finissi," Dr. Stowald said. The captain wore a flashy uniform with a white diagonal leather sash across a navy blue jacket and double gold buttons. A shiny gold motif lay on his hat.

Sandro looked at Cassandra with anxiety. He knew their hair could very well be on those uniforms. They moved on to the chamber of Parosius and Veturia.

"Mr. Taneschio, we seem to have a conundrum here. It appears two of our ancient Romans have achieved the improbable post-mortem ability to walk," Dr. Stowald said, pointing to a pair of skeletons whose right arms were now embraced—one on its back, the other on its stomach. "How do you suppose that could happen?" he asked.

Cassandra and Sandro were dumbfounded.

"I'm not following, Stowald. Everything looks to be in order from where I'm standing," Oliver interjected.

The professor walked over and stood next to Oliver. After pausing for a long moment, he removed his glasses and took another look around. "You know, you might be right, Oliver. Perhaps it was the angle I took yesterday that made their positions appear differently. I would suggest, however, that we never take such angles again," he said, glaring at Oliver, Cassandra, and Sandro. "But what of the records and photographs? Sandro, go to the lab and make sure the records are correct," he said with a blink.

Captain Finissi glanced at all of them with a skeptic eye and wrote in his notebook. "Dr. Stowald, what of this gold box you mentioned earlier?"

Turning to his old friend, he said, "Oliver, I'm afraid I have more bad news. Your box of Isis has also disappeared from our lab. I am truly sorry."

Oliver and Cassandra looked at the professor helplessly and felt as if someone had removed their souls.

The captain, a mustachioed fellow with thick eyebrows, scratched the side of his chin. He looked up from his note pad and stared at Professor Stowald with slight aggravation. He trusted the professor, but didn't like the notion that somebody might have tampered with archeological findings at Herculaneum. He took pride in enforcing the law and coming down hard when it came to artifacts. Moving a few bones around was something that he would take notice of on a slow day, but he had a bigger problem with a missing chest of Roman antiquities. They held not only significant historical value, but market value as well. Such artifacts could be worth millions, and he needed to find the culprits before they disappeared.

Sandro wiped his sweaty forehead with relief and much confusion. He took several pictures of the new chamber remains and headed back to the lab. Cassandra, also puzzled, followed him.

The Naples police took Sandro and Cassandra to headquarters. They were satisfied with the answers to their questions and released them shortly thereafter. The captain, in fact, was certain of their innocence in the matter, but wanted more information on Mee and Luke. Captain Finissi knew Luke Trettin. His people had been keeping an eye on him since he entered Italy. The name Luke Trettin was a fake, unlike Mee Lee who seemed to use her real name for this heist. The entire area, from Rome to Sorrento, was now on the lookout for Mee Lee and Mark Harston (Luke Trettin).

Sandro and Cassandra called a taxi to bring them back to the Herculaneum lab. With little time to spare before their bus in Rome was to bring the tour group to the airport, Cassandra gathered Oliver and kissed Sandro goodbye. As the cabbie turned to leave, Cassandra asked him to stop and quickly wrote her phone number and address on a piece of note paper. She then ran out and slipped the paper under the lab door. As she was about to leave, the door opened and she was pushed to the ground. Sandro laughed as he stooped to pick up the fallen American.

Oliver sat silently on the backseat of the cab while Cassandra said goodbye to Sandro. "I envy you, Sandro. There are so many stories to be told here in Herculaneum. Every day may be different than the next for you, but for me, I'll be back at my old job, selling suits. In a short time, Grandpa and I will be flying away from here and I don't like it."

"Is it only Herculaneum you'll miss?"

"Oh, I almost forgot. There's a tall, dark, Italian that I will need to talk to every now and then."

Sandro looked over at Oliver in the cab with a blank expression.

"She's talking about you, doctor", Oliver explained.

Sandro drew a cleansing breath and said, "I too don't want you to go." Then they kissed. It was a long, special kiss—like finally unmasking something beautiful that was hidden in a recurring dream. And now, just as they began to discover each other, they parted.

VESUVIUS

Sandro picked up Cassandra's phone number from the ground as the cab drove away.

17

Oliver and Cassandra watched Mount Vesuvius fade away as they drove toward Rome. It heaved a cloud of smoke to the sky as if to say it wasn't through with them. Cassandra's stomach turned slightly at the thought of another disaster. The cab dropped them in front of the hotel Pace-Helvezia where the tour bus was being filled and readied for their trip to the airport. The passengers talked of their visit to Sorrento and Napoli—about the beautiful scenery and the massive Angevin Castle. Cassandra sat back, half-listening and half-dreaming about Parosius, Veturia, and her new love, Sandro. Looking out the window, Cassandra watched as the proud Mount Vesuvius heaved another cloud of smoke to the sky.

Further down the street the bus rolled slowly past a police car with its lights flashing. The officers had Luke Trettin handcuffed. Mee Lee was nowhere in sight.

"One down, one to go!" Oliver noted.

"Do you think it was Mee?" Cassandra asked Oliver.

"Do I think 'what' was Mee?"

"Do you think she moved Parosius back with Veturia?"

"She's a liar and a thief. I'm not sure you want to know what I think."

"I think it was her. It was the way she looked at them. She wanted them together as much as I did. I think that the chests of artifacts may have been an after-thought."

Oliver looked at his granddaughter to check if she was serious. "That's some after-thought. Perhaps you're right, Cassandra, but she's a thief just the same."

As the tour bus entered the airport, Oliver became oblivious to anything going on around him. They boarded the plane and with his glasses down on the tip of his nose, he wrote his notes madly and as fast as his mind could think. Putting his pencil down, he waited for the plane to move. He looked straight ahead and wondered if he would ever be back. Cassandra sat dazedly, staring out the small plane window and suddenly realized her cell phone was ringing in her purse.

"Hello."

"Cassandra, it is Sandro. Look down, over by the ladder."

There he was, waving like a wild man and smiling.

"Goodbye, Cassandra. Will you remember me?"

She tapped on her grandfather's shoulder and pointed at Sandro.

"Of course, I'll remember you. Who knows, maybe I'll be back. You may need somebody to get you into trouble every now and then. Did you come all the way out here to see me off?"

"Well, yes…that and to tell you that you were right."

"Right…right about what?"

"The Roman woman, we found a bulla under her."

"Isn't that a young Roman's locket?"

"Yes, it contains an amulet as protection against evil. The name inscribed on it was *Fortunatus*."

Cassandra looked up to heaven. "Thank you, Sandro."

"That's not all. The ring under the big man's chest had an inscription as well. It was barely visible, but it said 'Veturia'."

Oliver overheard and sat with a look of great satisfaction over the completion of a mission that had started with a small box.

"One more thing—the woman, Veturia—we think she was pregnant. Our bone specialist, Sarah, checked it out. Arrivederci, Cassandra, and give my best to your grandfather."

"Sandro?"

"Yes, Cassandra."

"You could have called me from the lab, but I'm glad you came."

"Me too."

As the plane left the ground, Oliver, leaned back, his old Milwaukee Braves hat covering his eyes, and said, "He's the one."

"What do you mean?" Cassandra asked.

"Do you remember our agreement? You would pick a date for me, and I would pick your life partner...your soul-mate...your one-true-love."

"So you're picking him now? You're picking Sandro while we leave for America? Aren't you a bit off on the timing?"

"No, not in my estimation. He loves you, and it's easy to tell. But, a little distance will give you both the time you'll need to make smart decisions. Now go in the bathroom and sneak a call to him. The flight attendant won't bother you there."

"Getting mighty demanding, aren't you?"

"A deal's a deal. Now go on."

"You didn't exactly hold up your end of the bargain. I know you didn't have much time, but I didn't see you and…Ida, that was her name…Ida, making a night of it."

Oliver looked down about five rows and winked at Ida Nissen, who smiled shyly and winked back. "I wouldn't say that. After all, you weren't with me every minute."

Cassandra looked at the two, nodded, reached for her phone and walked back to the bathroom. Oliver made a motion for Ida to sit in the now vacant seat next to him. He knew that he and Ida could only be friends, but sometimes friends were hard to come by. He had plans that would not be compromised, and Ida was okay with that.

Oliver returned home on a warm, sunny day. His lineman-sized grandson, Jason, was seeding his garden. Jason greeted him with a bear hug, and together they walked to a well-maintained deck. There, Ted and Amy were sitting in patio chairs and enjoying tall glasses of ice tea.

"Looks like Jason lost a bet. One does the labor while the others sit back with a cool drink."

"To be fair, we've been taking turns," Amy insisted.

Jason wiped sweat from his forehead, "Yeah, I do the seeding and they decide who mixes the tea."

"Well, the garden looks great. We'll have fresh carrots and radishes in no time," Oliver said with a smile and a distant look in his eyes.

They told Oliver about a neighbor who had invited them to attend a party. This forced them to reciprocate. The resulting broken lamp was in a box in the front closet. A new one was now sitting on his living room end-table. Oliver offered them money for house-sitting, working the garden, and mowing the lawn. They refused, saying it had been payment enough to stay in his big house, compared to the cramped apartments they each lived in. As the sun set, they settled in to hear of Oliver's visit to Italy. He told them of the box of Isis, Cassandra's new boyfriend, and of Vesuvius. He spoke of Herculaneum and the skeletons that were found. The more he talked, the more he recalled and the more he needed to know. He told them to come back when his pictures were developed so he could give them a better explanation. He felt happy to be back home, surrounded by his family and friends, but something wasn't quite right. It was like when he'd sworn he put his reading glasses on the fireplace mantle, but they weren't there. He had an extra pair that worked just fine, but in the pit of his stomach the ache would not go away until he found the other pair.

After his grandchildren packed up and left, he stood alone in his den—alone again—just him and his books. Days later, looking at developed pictures of his trip with Cassandra, he knew what was missing. He knew what he needed to do. He would take his time and do it right.

The summer passed and most of fall. The air was cold, and Oliver could see his breath. Yesterday's snow didn't prevent him from entering Holy Angels Cemetery. He stood in front of a tombstone that said "Tessa Taneschio, 1933 – 1997." He had his suit coat on, and a cab was waiting for him. He had given his house keys to Jason and announced to all of his children and grandchildren that he was leaving and that any grandchild, that cared to, could rent out a bedroom for one dollar a month.

"I'm packed, Tessa. I don't know that I will be back. I'm going to miss our little talks. Watch over the kids for me." He knelt down…closer. "They say you can't teach an old dog, but I've learned something, Tessa. Remember, in grammar school, when the nuns always told us that God was everywhere? Well, I don't think He is. When we're hurting or when we're confused and don't know what to do, He's there. When young couples are blessed with a healthy child, He's there. When we pray to Him—if only to assure ourselves that we're not alone—He hears us, but He's not there all the time. He wasn't there when you died. He wasn't there last week when a young girl was raped and killed in Milwaukee. I expect He picks his battles. That's like you, Tessa. You're not just stationed right here where I'm kneeling. You can hear me—maybe not all the time, but you can hear me when I'm alone in bed and wishing you were there, or at the supermarket when I bring home chocolate ice-cream and realize chocolate was your favorite, not mine. And you'll hear me when I'm looking at our wedding picture on the bedside in Italy and singing our favorite song. I'll bet you're waiting for me right now."

After brushing his fingers gently over the engraved letters that spelled his late wife's name, he stood with moist eyes and walked sluggishly back to the cab. He knew he would never be back. He would miss his family, and they had expressed the same feeling the night before at a going-away party, but it was now or never.

Sandro called Cassandra nearly every other day since she left Italy. It made her days bright as she settled back into her modest Crystal River apartment. She now had plenty of time to figure out what she wanted to do with her life. She thought often about the people who had died under Vesuvius, especially Parosius and Veturia. Would Veturia have liked her? Was Parosius as courageous and handsome as her imagination had led her to believe? She thought of Sandro's first call when he told her of recovering nearly all of the boat chamber artifacts and about the arrest of Luke Trettin. All was found except the box of Isis, an old soldiers sword and of course, Mee Lee.

A week later the door bell rang as she was making dinner. She opened the door and with no one in sight, she looked down and saw a package was left behind. A box wrapped in plain brown paper held her address but did not have a return label. She ripped off the wrapping and lifted the box cover. Inside was another box, the golden box of Isis. Under the lid, she found a short note rolled on a small wooden dowel. The note was not of first century vintage, but very recent. The words were:

Cassandra,

Sorry about borrowing the pretty box without asking. You wouldn't believe what some people want to pay for this thing. I couldn't part with your old letters, but the golden box, may be better off in your hands.

Tell Oliver that I'm not finished yet! M.L.

The box was not damaged. Cassandra knew Mee Lee was taking a chance getting this to her. *I don't know what to think about that girl...and what did she mean by, "I'm not finished yet,"* she thought.

18

Months later, Cassandra joined her grandfather. A position had finally opened up working for the excavation lab in Herculaneum and she was thrilled. Sandro Ballantonio wasted no time pining for her attention—shortly after her arrival. They worked side-by-side, finding undisturbed artifacts and helping the world to understand how people lived nearly two-thousand years ago. Oliver became the official record keeper and couldn't have been happier. The embraced remains of Parosius and Veturia still rested on the beach of Herculaneum, together at last and forever.

On a warm July day, Sandro and Cassandra spread a blanket over a spot of lush green grass high above the Bay of Naples. The quiet parcel of land was little more than a mile north of Herculaneum. As a child, Sandro would picnic with his family on the very spot he rested with Cassandra. During their bike ride, Sandro pointed out the wooded areas along the way—each with its own happy past and perhaps joyous future with his American love. Sandwich and fruit were washed down with wine. Sandro hid a special find in their basket. He instructed his fiancée to cover her eyes.

"We can't keep her, but I wanted to show it to you before it went to the curator."

She opened her eyes to see a beautiful eight-inch marble figure.

"I uncovered it near the Villa of the Papyri."

"It is the most splendid Isis I've ever seen. I wish we could keep her."

This ancient artifact retained her color as if created yesterday. Her flesh-tone face held a smile, but her fingers were missing. The long gown looked flimsy in its light-blue hue. Her hands were raised palms-up in a gesture of praise. On its arm was an engagement ring.

Laying the goddess figure gently on the blanket, Sandro leaned toward Cassandra and kissed her. The kiss broke when, to the west, Vesuvius blew a sudden cloud of smoke. As if they were given a warning, the earth began to shake. It seemed to come from the bay— the waves moving violently. Their bottle of wine fell over as they jumped to their feet. Sixty feet above the sea, the tall bank started to drop. They ran madly, away from the sea. Looking back Cassandra saw the statue of Isis fall over and roll downward. She dove for it, but missed. The ring rolled off the arm of Isis just before the statue fell down the cliff. Sandro dove for the ring and snatched it. He turned over, dropped it in his pocket and saw that Cassandra was beginning to slide down the steep drop. Sandro reached and grasped her hand.

Give me your other hand," Sandro said grimacing.

Cassandra did just that.

He pulled her up, and they scrambled away from the danger. They held each other tight, their faces caked with dirt. Just then, as the rumbling began to subside, Sandro knelt down on one knee.

"I was planning on a more romantic setting, but this will have to do. Cassandra, will you do me the honor of being my wife?"

Her exuberance was, perhaps, a bit too much as she jumped into his arms and nearly tossed them both over the newly formed cliff. Sandro reached into his pant pocket and breathed a sigh of relief when he discovered the ring was still there. He finally put it on her finger.

Just as fast as the quake came, it stopped. From the lab the tremor was mild, but it did get Oliver and Doctor Stowald's attention. They ran out of the building to see if there was any damage. From a distance, they could see Sandro and Cassandra running towards them.

"Are you all right?" Oliver shouted in a panicked voice.

"We're fine. We're better than fine," Cassandra said looking at her left hand.

"As long as both of you are safe, that's all that matters," the doctor replied. "What's wrong, you both look strange."

Cassandra showed them the ring.

"It's about time," Oliver said sternly, then smiled. "I couldn't be happier."

"I'm happy for you both," Stowald followed.

"A sizable plot of land dropped down towards the bay, I'm afraid it took a few things with it—our transportation—as well as the statue of Isis, Sandro found yesterday," Cassandra admitted.

"And what were you doing with such a find on your lunch hour?" Doctor Stowald asked. "Never mind, we'll worry about that later. The Vesuvius Observatory will let us know when it is safe to look over the area. Until then, we'll need to be patient."

Cassandra could only wonder what her marriage would be like with this kind of a start.

The next day a call to the seismologist told them the quake was quite strange. It was centralized in one small area. It measured a magnitude of little more than a three with minor aftershocks. The intensity scale recorded a five at the center. It was as if a small bomb had been set off from within the earth at a very concentrated spot.

The crew at Herculaneum meticulously checked the ancient ruins for damage, while Sandro and Cassandra brought Dr. Stowald and Oliver to the area where they had picnicked the day before. Standing on a bank set back some fifty feet thanks to the quake, they looked down and discovered that much of the broken ground had indeed rumbled into the sea.

"Merda Santa...ah...forgive me, but look," Sandro shouted pointing below.

Like shiny boulders protruding through a muddy river, huge white pillars shown through the broken soil. Finding a jagged path down to the site, Sandro and Cassandra quickly descended with the two old men slowly following behind them. They stared with mouths gasping. The entrance to a villa was easy to see. The rest was still well under the very ground and volcanic rock they had stood on only moments ago. Sandro stepped forward, but was held back by Stowald.

"I know it's hard, but we need to approach this like any other find. Besides, you nearly stepped on this."

He reached down and dug around a pair of small hands that poked out of the ground. Upright as if standing guard, the goddess, Isis, was uncovered and picked up, gently.

"It's her...it is Isis. She still has a little magic, does she not?" Sandro grinned, looking intently at the goddess.

"The goddess of rebirth felt it was time to unearth a hidden treasure," Oliver said, looking at what appeared to be the entrance of a villa.

The magnificent structure was covered with a mixture of earth and rock—unlike the cemented flow of Herculaneum. Removing the debris proved to be even easier than they had expected, but not without danger and obstacles. All available excavators turned their attention to this ancient resort villa and continued their labor, day and night.

Weeks later, nearly half of the villa was uncovered. The work was dangerous with built in obstacles and falling rock. The atrium's marble pool showed several cracks, but was otherwise in good shape. Colorful wall and floor mosaics of gods, as well as those of outdoor life, appeared after each room was reasonably safe to enter.

Sandro, his face covered in dirt, mixed with sweat, put a call to the lab from within the villa. "You'd better come, sir."

"How many times have I told you to call me Oliver? What do you have?"

"It's a wall painting of a family. I think we may have found the owners."

Oliver moved quickly. He jumped into a four-wheeler, and moments later stood by his future grandson-in-law. "I can't believe it. It's them. It's the family of Veturius Fortunatus." Oliver examined a wall painting depicting Veturius, his wife Livia, his daughter Veturia, and son Crescentius. They stood together in a sunny field of tall grass and wildlife. In the background were the heavenly caricatures of ancestors. The Fortunatus family names were chiseled into the wall below.

"There's more!" Sandro said.

Shaking with excitement, Oliver followed Sandro through the bedrooms and into a newly dug tablinum, used as a recreation room. A large wooden desk with one pull-out drawer was still intact. Before the desk was a masterfully built marble chair secured to the floor. The chair was tall and structured to allow a short man to do his writing comfortably. Its color was a dark-green mixed with clouds. *The heat of the rock must have destroyed any cushion material that may have been used on the cold, hard chair,* Oliver thought. It was then that he remembered, "The gem of the pharaoh lies beneath your chair of honor." *This could be Veturius' chair of honor.* He knelt down but the chair was boxed in on all four sides. He pushed on each panel until he felt something give...just a little. "Give me a hand, Sandro!"

They pushed hard, but something seemed to be holding it back.

"It could be a weight mechanism," Dr. Stowald volunteered from a distance as he limped into the room with Cassandra at his side.

"What do you mean, Stowald?"

"The Roman elite were quite fond of having personal hiding places. If they found the right builders or engineers, the designs became very elaborate."

Oliver got to his feet. "What do you suggest?"

"Take a seat, Sandro," the doctor said feeling for something under the arm rest. "Ah yes, here it is." He pressed a square cut-out, but nothing happened. "It may be based on the weight of the chair's owner and can only be re-adjusted by the builder. A pyramid shaped rock is built with his exact weight. Should the owner's weight fluctuate, the heavy scalene would be used in his place. I expect Sandro's weight would be well over that of the average Roman from the first century. Let's search for such a suitable replacement."

As they scattered, Oliver continued his examination of the chair. At one hundred and sixty-five pounds, Oliver was at least forty pounds lighter than Sandro. He sat cautiously in Veturius' chair and reached under the arm-rest. Suddenly a clicking sound preceded a *whoosh* from beneath the chair. The panel sprang out, revealing a hidden drawer. Sandro ran to Oliver, knelt, and reached inside. He pulled out a square gold box. In the box, on a piece of fine cloth, unscathed by the heat of the volcanic surge, lay an amazingly large gray pearl with a deep-pink tint. It was set in gold, and as they all gathered in awe, they realized they were in the presence of the grandest pear shaped earring any of them had ever seen.

"The gem of the Pharaoh is a pearl!" Cassandra said in a voice barely over a whisper.

Doctor Stowald took the piece from Sandro and adjusted his glasses. Oliver sat up, startled, as the drawer sprang back into its hidden position. He looked over his friend's shoulder to see what had attracted everyone's attention.

"Steve, you don't think it could be…no…highly unlikely…but still."

The doctor looked at Oliver and then again at the gem. "I don't know whether to be more shocked at this beautiful pearl or at the fact that you called me by my first name."

"It sure looks like it could be the real thing. The size...it's unbelievable."

"If you're referring to the earring of Cleopatra, you may be right."

"What are you two talking about?" Cassandra inquired.

The doctor spoke to one of his workers in Italian and asked him to retrieve his laptop from the laboratory. "It is a long and very old story, but one that is true. A historian by the name of Pliny the Elder wrote about an examination he had concluded around AD 72 on a single pearl earring that had once belonged to Cleopatra."

Oliver joined in, "Originally two pearl earrings were given to Cleopatra by Queen Candace of Kush as a gift to seal her alliance with Egypt. After the death of Mark Antony and Queen Cleopatra, Augustus Ceasar became the sole ruler of the Roman Empire. Mark Antony's adjutant, the tribune Lucius Plautus remained loyal to Julius Caesar, and after the latter's assassination, to Mark Antony. Plautus bargained his life and those of his fellow officers by agreeing to present the renowned earrings to Augustus. It is said he retrieved but one earring from the dead body of Mark Antony."

"That explains one earring. What about the other?"

Doctor Stowald continued, "That's where it gets sticky. If you believe the stories that Pliny wrote, one earring was destroyed and the other cut in two and reshaped so that a jewel could rest in each of the ears of the statue of Venus in the Pantheon at Rome. It is alleged that the remaining whole pearl was dropped into a vessel of vinegar by orders of Cleopatra. The vinegar was said to have broken down the pearl, whereby Cleopatra swallowed the concoction while a curious Marc Antony looked on. Because pearls were associated with the goddess Venus, it was written that Cleopatra did this as an aphrodisiac."

"Pearls are not very hard, but their make-up of mostly calcium carbonate makes them quite strong. Pliny wrote that the pearl he examined was the size of a large dove's egg. They are hard to break. For Cleopatra to dissolve and drink the combination, the gem would have had to be crushed first. Many find that part of the story a bit hard to believe," Oliver said, moving aside as a worker by the name of Mitros handed Steve his laptop.

The doctor opened a file of a sketch based on Pliny the Elder's description. It looked very much like the treasure they now held.

"Is the cut pearl still around?"

"No, Cassandra, it was last seen and reported stolen around 1540. There hasn't been a trace of it since."

"If this is the pearl of Cleopatra, what would something like this be worth?" Sandro asked.

"In Pliny's day the value for the pearl was worth 160,000 aureus. Today, it's off the charts," Steve estimated.

"That's what I was waiting to hear," a short worker in overalls, a back-pack, and a stocking hat said. She held a bright silver pistol and pointed it at the doctor. The workers outside had gone for lunch, leaving the intruder with five captives.

"Mee? Mee Lee, is that you?" asked an incredulous Cassandra.

"You got it, Cassy. The locals were talking up a rumor about an ancient villa find. I've been keeping a close eye on this place ever since. It looks like my patience paid off," she said, dazzled at the enormity of the pearl that rested in Steve Stowald's palm. "I'll have that pearl, Doctor." He dropped it carefully into Mee's hand. Mee, grinning from ear-to-ear, gently dropped it into the gold box.

"Miss Lee, I have two questions; how can you possibly expect to leave Italy with a gem this size and not be apprehended, and who would pay a worthy price on such a stolen historically significant piece?" Oliver asked.

"Not that it's any of your business, but I've escaped Italy's grasp once before and I can do it again. As for a buyer...there's always a buyer." Mee looked back and noticed the unfinished adjoining room. "What's in there?"

"It's an oecus or entertainment room. The room is not cleared and too dangerous to excavate at this time," Doctor Stowald explained.

Mee heard a noise outside the entrance and quickly ran out to check on it. There she found a worker who had come back early from his break.

"You'll do nicely. What's your name little fellow?" Mee asked.

"Mmm...Mitros."

"Well, Mmmmitros, come on in."

Mee ordered Mitros to remove the flashlight from his belt and shine it into the four foot opening. The entrance to the oecus was broad enough for all to enter, as long as they stepped in one at a time. Mitros, who was even shorter than Mee, would have little trouble. She pushed Mitros into the room and poked her head inside briefly, while still holding her gun on her captives. "You've been holding out doctor. At a glance, I'd say my work is not finished." She pointed her weapon at a lantern. "Cassy, pick up that lantern and follow your friends inside."

"Are you sure you want to do that, Mee? We could all be injured or worse," Oliver said stopping at the opening.

"I'll take that chance." Mee entered and let her eyes adjust to the dim light—her jaw dropped. A marble altar partially entombed by molten rock was flanked by identical statues of Mercury, the fleet-footed god of commerce. The few small openings on the floor, not covered in soil and rock, revealed a colorful mosaic that must have covered the entire room. There were large plant holders and vases all painted in vibrant gold. Mee momentarily forgot about her captives who stood huddled together just inside the entrance. Her eyes moved from one treasure to another. Oliver and the others made no attempt to flee. They were aware of the riches this room held and of the danger they were in without proper precautions. A sudden move or a loud noise could cause the heavy rock from above to drop. Worse yet, elite Romans of the day were not above setting traps to protect their valuables. Mee moved around a corner and stopped suddenly when her eyes closed in on a life-sized statue. There, in all its glory, stood the goddess Isis. Buried from the waist down, one arm was held out as if blessing the villa. The goddess was masterfully depicted in a sheer gown. Mee found she was surrounded by more riches than any self-respecting thief could hope for. Most of what she saw was too big to carry on her own—marble tables, gold pots, and large silver planters—until she saw a magnificent piece around the neck of Isis. The necklace was triangular and dazzled in brilliance, despite the harsh surroundings. Hundreds of sapphire and diamonds were held together by a rich thread of gold. "I...I'm going to need that," Mee stuttered.

She walked slowly toward the goddess, unable to take her eyes off the necklace. "You...you crawl up there and remove that necklace. She won't need it anymore," Mee ordered Mitros.

Mitros was back with the others and muttered something in Latin to Sandro. His expression, wrought with fear, when he took slow, calculated steps toward the life-size statue. With Mee right behind him, he inched ever closer to the angelic goddess. The tall figure seemed to be looking down upon him. Her features were in the Archaic Greek style. Her nose was prominent and she looked to be a model of feminine strength. Isis wore a long headdress and her gown seemed to be shear. Mitros, now only a foot away, turned to scale the rocks just to the left side of the goddess. After taking one more step, a clicking sound was heard. Mitros backed up and looked around in quick jerks. Barely a breath could be heard.

"Go on!" Mee pushed the pistol into his back.

Abruptly the ceiling began to rumble. A thick, curved wall began to fall from above. Mitros dove away from the stone divider, but the bottom half of his legs did not make it in time. The wall's descent was slowed and then stopped by debris, only inches from the floor, saving Mitros' legs from being crushed. Black dust billowed everywhere as Sandro pulled Mitros up and away. Loose rock from above started to fall. The curved wall now stood before the goddess, protecting it from intruders. All six who entered the room retreated hurriedly—all except Mee. She looked desperately to find a way to the goddess and the treasure around her neck before more rock fell. By the time she realized there were no clear paths to Isis, her only exit was gone.

"Mee...are you okay?" Cassandra asked from her safe haven outside the oecus. A small ten-inch opening remained.

Mee, down on the ground, bloodied from fallen debris, was trapped in the now darkened room. "Get me out of here or I swear I'll crush this pearl under a rock!"

Cassandra looked at Oliver and smiled. "You're in no position to give orders, Mee. Drop your gun and throw the pearl out here and we'll think about getting you out of there."

After a long moment of silence, Mee's hand reached through the opening, handing over the items.

"How did you know she wouldn't destroy the pearl?" Oliver asked Cassandra.

"When she returned the box of Isis I knew she was the type that felt strong about anything of antiquity."

"You took a shot, didn't you?"

"Yes!"

"You're right, Cassandra. You had me figured out," Mee's voice echoed from the dark room. "But, I know something you don't."

"And what might that be?"

"The burned scroll from the golden box of Isis—I know what the missing part is."

"What missing part?" Oliver interrupted.

There was a long pause and some shuffling of feet could be heard. "Give me a few minutes to think about it. I'm not sure I'm ready to tell you anything."

Dr. Stowald decided it would be more humane to get her out of there as quickly as possible. The workers began to remove the debris. Oliver could hear Mee moving around the room. The opening was soon large enough to allow Mee to crawl out of her self-imposed prison when the sound of falling rock echoed from within. Cassandra called out for Mee, but there wasn't a reply. When the workers finally got inside the oecus they found Mee across the room lying on the floor and unresponsive. She may have been looking for another way out and disturbed some loose rock. Her head was bleeding in the back. Oliver crawled in and tied his handkerchief around her head. She was quickly carried out of the dangerous room.

Oliver raised her head slightly and poured water on her dust filled face to clear the dirt. Mee responded by weakly opening her eyes.

"You're hurt pretty bad, Mee. We've called for medics. They should be here soon."

Mee looked at Oliver. It was a serious, scared look. Oliver's handkerchief was now a deep red. He took off his shirt and held it tight to her head.

"I'm not sure the medics will be able to help much, Oliver. Could you hold me for a while?"

Oliver propped her up against his chest and held her as she had asked.

"I need to tell you something, Oliver. I've been obsessed with your golden box for about twelve years now."

"Twelve years…you couldn't have been more than fourteen," Oliver guessed.

"My family lived in Madison for a couple of years. I was thirteen. My parents sent me to a school for gifted students...down in Chicago. My brother, Chue, stayed in town and was in your class that year. He told me about the box that you displayed during his Roman history course. Chue was not the type to get excited about things, but he did that day. His eyes were big when he told me about the box that weekend. I was jealous. I convinced him to get me pictures of the box and the scrolls. I don't know how he did it, but he did. I did his homework for the entire semester as pay back. I still have those pictures."

Mee coughed and spit up some blood.

"You should stop talking," Oliver urged Mee.

"It's a little late to be worrying about me now, Oliver. Where were you ten years ago?"

Oliver thought back, "We didn't have much diversity in race back then. I would have remembered your brother and I don't recall a Chue Lee." His voice trembled as he said the name. Something didn't feel right deep inside of his stomach.

"My brother died when he was a freshman in college. He had a different father than I did. His name was Chue Park."

Oliver's face began to pale. Cassandra was confused.

Mee's face revealed a look of hatred. "An old woman had a heart attack on Lakeshore Drive, just off the campus. It was a snowy, winter night. You remember, don't you Oliver?"

"Stop," Oliver demanded, but with little command.

"She skid over the center-line and hit my brother's car head on. He was killed instantly. My parents never recovered and divorced soon after. When Chue died it was as if my family didn't exist."

Cassandra now understood and turned away.

"It wasn't her fault. Tessa was…it…it just happened," Oliver whispered.

"I didn't get a chance to say goodbye, but you did. I had no one to blame…no one to be mad at. I was owed something. The emptiness had to be filled. I wanted to find what your grandfather couldn't."

Oliver held Mee tighter. "I could have helped. You should have come to me. We could have helped each other. Months later, after Tessa past away, I tried to contact your parents, but I was told they had moved. I wanted to see if I could do something."

Mee's eyes were losing focus and she started to shiver uncontrollably.

"It was just by chance you know. I went to the University of Michigan and I found it. It was a perfect match," Mee said faintly.

"Found what?" Cassandra asked.

Mee's head turned and she began to lose consciousness just as the ambulance reached them.

"1893…1893," Mee whispered before blacking out.

As Oliver gently carried her to the emergency vehicle, a necklace holding a strange looking key, slid off to Mee's right side.

19

Oliver was not a man who could let an unsolved mystery rest. His shock at the revelation of Mee's tragic connection to him only fueled his need to find answers. Mee may have found solutions to the equations left behind in his grandfather's golden box. What did she know? What did she mean by '1893' or was it just gibberish caused by her head injury? He felt the weight of generations needed to be lifted. If God would give him enough time, perhaps he could sift through the secrets of the past and finally end what his grandfather couldn't.

It was of no use to ask Mee. The doctors at the hospital, 'Cardinal Ascalesi' were doubtful that she would regain consciousness. He started by backtracking the footsteps of Mee Lee's life. The more he uncovered, the more he began to be impressed with her mind and abilities. A search for her latest residence came up with a small apartment in Naples. Hotel records showed she had been there for about a month under a different name. He told the front desk that she had been in a severe accident and as a friend was hoping he could be allowed in her room to look for family phone numbers. They obliged and Oliver was able to give Mee's mother the news on the state of her daughter. He left out his connection to the family and Mee's current career path. He also found enough information to discover that Mee's recent past pointed to Ann Arbor, Michigan.

With an address found in her purse, it only took a few phone calls to find that she had convinced a professor at the University of Michigan that she held a doctorate in papyrology, and requested to study their library-housed papyri.

It took some convincing, but Oliver was able to take Cassandra and Sandro away from their marriage plans. He booked tickets to Bishop International and they landed in Michigan the next day. An hour later, they found themselves in room 807 of the Harlan Hatcher Graduate Library at the center of the University of Michigan campus.

The Associate Professor of Papyrology, Terry Gragori looked up from his desk as they approached. "You must be, Mr. Taneschio."

"Oliver...call me Oliver, and I've brought a couple of colleagues from our lab," Oliver said introducing Sandro and Cassandra. "I hope you don't mind."

The professor asked his three visitors to address him as, Grago, as his colleagues affectionately do, and then said, "Come, I'm excited to show you around. After you called I did some checking on Mee Lee. From what you told me, I wish I had been more efficient with our security when young Mee Lee was here. She did have realistic looking credentials. I have to give her credit for being prepared."

"That sounds like Mee. Her life didn't turn out...that is...she could have been a great person if things have gone a different way." Oliver needed to somehow defend Mee, because no one else would. He understood she was capable of making her own decisions, but Oliver was feeling that much of what happened to Mee was because of his own failing. He didn't do enough to help her when she was young, but he could do something now.

The library was filled with rows where stacks of books, dissertations, monographs, and of course editions of papyri were shelved. Professor Gragori led them to row two, a large combination of literary and biblical papyri editions. The natural lighting was very bright, coming from three large windows in the back of the room. Oliver loved the smell of old literature and smiled as he looked at the multitude of historic information. As the three visitors scanned the books, Oliver asked Gragor, "Does the number '1893' mean anything to you professor?"

He thought about it for awhile and finally said, "I think that may have been Mee's inventory number. Yes…I'm quite sure," he said looking down at the check in/out list on his desk.

"What do you mean inventory number—inventory for what?" Cassandra asked.

"It's our ancient papyri collection. Each text, each fragment, is kept in our vault, and every piece has its own inventory number. Mee was here for only a few day's, but '1893' was the only piece of papyrus she was interested in."

Sandro looked down at the shorter, curly haired professor. "Can you show us this papyrus?"

Just outside the library and down the hall was a steel door. Next to that a locked climate control displayed the reading of 65° and 45% of relative humidity. The professor opened the door only to reveal an inner, sealed door. Dim lights were activated as he opened the second door and entered the vault. His three new students watched with mounting curiosity as he opened a metal cabinet and slid out a thin pair of 8 by 10 inch pieces of glass. From Oliver's vantage point he could see it housed a papyrus.

"Much of our stronger fragments are stored in special folders, but those of this age and tenderness we house them in glass," Grago said in low and controlled voice. "This is odd," he continued looked at the glass casing. We edge the panels with a material that lets air through. This looks like it has been tampered with."

He took the panel out to the library for a better look. As he did Cassandra and Oliver gasped at the same time.

"Cassandra, do you see? It is our artifact, the note from Veturius Fortunatus. It seems you have been a victim of a switch, Grago."

Looking intently at the fragment, Grago said, "This is not good. We've never had anything like this happen before. What can you tell me of this piece, Oliver? "

"It was believed to be written between AD 79 and AD 81—a type of confession from a Roman to his missing daughter. Can you tell me what was originally between the two pieces of glass?"

"Oddly, it was a fragment from around the same time period. Only a small number of words were visible. I think the top half was burned."

Sandro walked to the set of windows and looked out at the multitude of campus buildings shining in the bright sun. "Grago, would you happen to know where Mee was staying while she was in Ann Arbor?"

"As a matter of fact, she sub-leased an apartment just outside campus. One of my grad students, Adam, took a liking to Miss Lee and set her up. If you're thinking of going there, I wouldn't mind driving. I'm sure Adam can get us in to see it. He's very resourceful."

All four packed themselves into Grago's fuel efficient automobile and headed down South State. Hanging a right on Hill Street, they stopped in the middle of the block where a white apartment building that seemed to be standing on stilts rested. They parked under the structure and entered through two large glass doors. Just inside, Grago's high-strung, and stately grad student was waiting.

Adam Winterfeldt, was a pocket size young man with crazy blond hair and a bright yellow bow tie. He had a strange way of whispering the last word or two of each sentence. "I have a master *key*. I kind of look after the place...the place. The landlord gives me a break on the rent...rent."

Adam led the way upstairs to an efficiency apartment on the south side of the complex. He unlocked the door and said, "She'll be angry with me if she finds out I let you in. You can look, but don't touch...don't touch."

Professor Gragori looked down at his fidgety student. "I'm afraid it doesn't appear that she will be coming back, Adam. She's gravely ill."

"That...is most...disappointing...disappointing," Adam said in a whisper. His exuberance disappeared and was replaced with a lost, distant look.

"Well then, there you are. I'll be off. Lock it when you're finished...finished."

Cassandra watched him leave with his head down and feet shuffling, as if in a hurry to hide his emotions. She wondered if his obvious affection for Mee was reciprocated or completely one sided. Professor Gragori ran to check on his student.

The apartment consisted of a room with a bath, kitchen, and dining table on one end and a bed on the other. Oliver flipped a wall switch that turned on a lamp that rested on a small computer desk at the end of a twin-sized bed. On the desk was a laptop computer.

Cassandra sat on a well used wooden chair and opened it. Once powered up, the desktop icons revealed a number of interesting files.

While the others checked cabinets, drawers, boxes, and closets, Cassandra dug into files that she had hoped would reveal the path that Mee Lee was taking before her accident. Most of the files were fact finding research on Herculaneum and the surrounding area. There were maps, Roman history, and archeological findings...everything she needed for the study of ancient artifacts along the Naples and Almafi coast. But one file, simply called *Oliver*, divulged perhaps more than she wanted to know.

It started out with a quote from Lucius Annaeus Seneca written in the middle of the 1st century:

"Dangerous is wrath concealed. Hatred proclaimed doth lose its chance of wreaking vengeance."

"Received an interesting reply from Pietro Giovanni" Mee keyed in. The following e-mail was copied to her letter:

Thank you for your kind words Miss Lee. I checked our archives concerning a gift given to one, Demetri Taneschio, around the end of the 19th century. There seems to be a bit of confusion. Mr. Taneschio had indeed worked in excavation for many years, but he was dropped from his employment just before his retirement. The gold box you speak of was finely made to be sure, but such a golden covered box was given to many of the workers upon retirement. It was manufactured around 1890. As far as the papyri that you detailed so thoroughly in your letter, there is a note in the records that describes fragments that were discovered, but that disappeared. They were found under an ancient villa in Rome. Demetri Taneschio was dismissed of his supervisory position under suspicion of artifact theft.

Despite the theft, he was given the golden box for his years of work. It was noted that any remaining pieces from the Roman villa were kept in our Naples museum until 1922. At that time, a Mr. J.W. Anderson acquired a substantial amount of early Roman documents for the University of Michigan Institute of Archaeological Research. Your fragment may well have been included in that transaction.

Good luck with your search, Miss Lee. I know you contend that the missing pieces are not available to you, but please keep in mind that if you should find these fragments, they are the property of the Italian government. Of course a monetary award may be yours should they be recovered.

Pietro Giovanni – Superintendent of Archaeology – Vesuvius.

"Cassandra, have you found anything of value?" Oliver asked as he looked through a closet.

"No…nothing of value…just data on archaeology," Cassandra answered. She could not tell her grandfather what she read. She turned away from Oliver, printed out the letter, and deleted the file.

"Questo è lo," Sandro whispered as he stood in front of an old built-in bookcase. "Oliver, I have found it."

Sandro held a realistic looking, but phony bible. The bible was actually a wooden box with a white cover, back and binding with gold lettering and page ends. After opening the cover, a silver wine cup rested gently on fine cloth. Under that a glass, like those in the archeological library, lay inside.

Sandro took out the cup and reached carefully to remove the glass. Between the two pieces of glass there were ancient fragments. Oliver stared intently at the artifacts.

"She did it, Cassandra, come look. She put the puzzle together. The bottom fragment she found at the library fits together perfectly with the other half that my grandfather held so many years in the golden box.

Oliver read the translation out loud. *"The chest of Janus holds a sword marked Petros. It is special to Parosius. Keep it safe for his return."*

Your loving daughter, Veturia

Oliver sat and thought about what he had read. Looking up at the empty spot where the bible had been he noticed an odd cup. He reached for it and adjusted his glasses.

"What is it, Oliver?" Sandro asked.

"The pearl of Cleopatra was just a bonus. Mee was after something bigger, something I always thought was a story. What a fool I've been. She was after the sword...the sword of Peter."

20

"It would appear my grandfather knew more than he let on. He knew about the sword. He used to tell us stories about it when I was a child. I thought of it as a bedtime story...something he made up. How could he have known it was real?" *He would have to have had both pieces of papyri,* Oliver thought.

Oliver looked knowingly at Cassandra. "You hesitated when I asked you if you found anything on Mee's laptop. Did Mee find something that would explain this?"

Cassandra saw hurt in Oliver's eyes, but knew he would find the truth eventually. She handed him the letter she printed from the Vesuvius Superintendent of Archaeology.

Oliver read the letter and set it aside.

"It doesn't mean anything. There could be many reasons why he took the artifacts. Maybe they treated him badly," Cassandra reasoned.

"Oh, I think it means a great deal, Cassandra. It means my grandfather hid the truth from his family. For whatever reason, he chose to steal from those that employed him and he died alone. Thanks to Mee I at least know why he became obsessed. It was the sword."

Grasping the wine cup he reached inside his suit coat and examined it with a small magnifying glass. The cup was magnificent in its detail, but had a scuffed, almost dirty appearance.

"The creases are still encrusted with debris," Oliver mumbled. In the center of the two-handled cup was the image of a Roman. Below the man was the name of 'Parosius'. He held a sword. The handle of the sword was formed with what appeared to be a fish head.

"The night Mee and her blond friend broke into the beach site they moved the skeletons of Parosius and Veturia. I think she found this cup under Parosius. Once she put the fragments together, she began to see that the sword was the true prize. The wine cup is just further proof of its existence."

"How did the fragments get separated," Cassandra asked.

"I think my grandfather found the fragments when they were together. He kept the translation to himself and broke the letter in two parts. He may have had enough time to hide some of it, but was caught with the rest. He was subsequently asked to retire and kept the secret with him ever since."

Oliver looked at the fragments once more. "Sandro, I'm not familiar with the name 'Janus'. Can you tell me anything about such a name?"

"It may be in reference to the Roman God. Janus was their God of gates and doors. It also stood for new beginnings. Its appearance was...ahh...how you say...shown...deepi..."

"Depicted?" Cassandra guessed.

"Yes...generally depicted with two faces, looking in the opposite directions. One face was meant for what was left behind...the other looked toward what lies ahead. But Oliver, I did not see such a thing in the villa."

"You're right, Sandro, perhaps such a chest is not in the villa. Suffice to say, however, if we find the chest, we find the sword. If Mee came upon the cup under Parosius then it is not a stretch to believe she may have found the key that was around her neck under Veturia." Oliver felt the ancient key that was now resting on his chest.

Oliver thought a while more. "I don't think Mee was looking for an escape route when she was hurt. I think she was looking for whatever holds the sword."

"Oliver, what of the sword? What story did your grandfather tell you?" Sandro asked.

Oliver scratched his head and thought back. "It always began with the story of St. Peter in the garden of Gethsemane, just like in the bible. Jesus was being arrested when Simon Peter drew his sword and used it to cut off the ear of a servant who was employed by a high priest. If memory serves, the slaves name was, Malchus. Jesus would have none of it and told Peter to put the sword back into the sheath. Although any mention of the sword in the bible seems to end there, my grandfather's stories continued well beyond the time of Jesus."

"How come you never talked about your grandfathers stories before?" Cassandra asked as she walked back to Mee's computer.

"Before today the stories were just that, stories. Now they mean something. Now there is a connection to how Demetri acted…how he lived his life."

"So go on, tell of the sword," Sandro said as if he would not tolerate another interruption.

"After the episode in the garden, the sword was passed to many a Christian. Whenever a Christian was in possession of the sword he became protected. After Jesus was crucified there were many bad years for his followers. The sword became not a symbol to be worshipped, but a force that was once used to protect Jesus and was now a cloak to preserve the remaining Christians," Oliver said pausing briefly. He looked at Sandro and noticed his intensity.

"This story seems to have drawn your interest."

"It is not unlike some of the stories I've heard from my own family, perhaps told for many centuries. Please Oliver, continue."

"Well, let's see. Grandfather told us boys many stories of how each Christian used the sword to his benefit. Each story went farther into the first century. I can't tell you how many times we would pester him to tell us more when we came home from school. I remember when I was eight years old; things between my father and grandfather were coming to a boiling point. It was 1938 and the 'Pact of Steel' between Italy and Germany was completed. This was the last straw for my father. He told us we were packing up and shipping to America within a couple of weeks. We were, my brother and I, a little too young to realize that we were going to be permanently separated from grandfather. We thought of it as more of a vacation. Before we left we begged him to finish the story of Peter's sword."

Cassandra stopped scanning Mee's computer and sat next to Oliver.

"He told us that the sword survived the years until the time Peter was arrested in Rome. He had been imprisoned for about seven months in some awful dark hole of a cell, when he escaped. As he walked along the road, Jesus appeared and told him his destiny was to return. He turned and headed back to the prison. As he walked awhile longer, a stranger met him. The stranger handed him his old sword...a sword he hadn't seen in over thirty years. The sword was special to him in many ways. It was given to him by his own father and he used it on his fishing boat to slash and cut fish. But, despite its history, he told the stranger that he didn't need it where he was going. The stranger was to see that it got to Peter's wife and daughter. Although there are differing views from scholars on his time of death, I believe the evidence points to early AD 68. He was said to have asked to be crucified upside down because he was not worthy to be crucified in the same manner as Jesus," Oliver said as he paused for a moment.

"Is that the last of it? What happened to the sword during the eleven years between his death and eruption of Vesuvius?" Cassandra asked.

"All grandfather ever said was that it was last seen near Vesuvius. It waits to be discovered, because the stories of the sword must never end. Until now I didn't know what my grandfather was so adamant about. Why would he stay and search while his family left him. Now I know why. It doesn't excuse his behavior, but at least it explains it."

21

The wedding of Doctor Sandro Ballantonio and Cassandra Taneschio was delayed a couple of weeks in order to accommodate the bride's wishes. This gave Oliver his chance to look deeply into the evidence at hand concerning the sword of St. Peter. He wanted to find the relic in the worst way and Cassandra was starting to worry about her grandfather. Was he beginning to obsess over this? Oliver told her it was about closure...closure for his grandfather, Demetri and closure for Mee. Still, he wasn't sleeping and eating well, and he began to look pale and tired. Cassandra felt he was turning into Demetri. The more he studied his findings and searched, the more frustrated he became and, yet, determined to continue. *Perhaps the wedding will take his mind from the sword, if only for a short time,* she thought.

It took the government and many skilled workers and volunteers to pull it off, but the end result was truly one-of-a-kind. The villa looked amazing. Father John Pucci agreed to participate in this highly unconventional wedding celebration on one condition. They were to wed during a short mass in his church prior to the ceremony in the villa. Afterwards, he would follow Sandro and Cassandra to the villa to take part in their big night.

The Villa of Fortunatus proved to be the exquisite gem that Cassandra imagined it to be. The garden held the perfect setting for the future Mrs. Ballantonio. Professor Stowald pulled a lot of strings to allow for the use of the villa as the wedding site. The colonnaded court was cleaned to its original powder white and the garden was adorned with potted greenery. Torches made of pitch-pine were lit per

Roman tradition and placed throughout the court. Nearly all of Oliver's children and grandchildren made the trip from America, some, stretching their credit card to the limit. The bride's party was dwarfed however, by the groom's hardy family. They came from all of Italy to celebrate the union. On this day, most were dressed as ancient Romans. Those men who chose to do as the Romans did, sported white togas with purple borders, while the women wore flowing light-purple gowns with ornate necklaces, pins, and bracelets. Sandro looked striking in his dark purple toga with gold trim.

A pre-mass ceremony was held before a likeness of the god of weddings, Hymen Hymenaeus. Cassandra explained to their priest that it was in honor of those that were not able to wed when Vesuvius buried their hopes and dreams. In Hymen's outstretched hands lay the pearl of Cleopatra. Standing at each side were, understandably, museum security guards. An ancient wedding song was sung to Cassandra by small girls dressed as Lares in knee-high tunics, who danced around her and attended to her needs. The songstress sang in a poetic voice that spoke of good omens and the blessings of Hymen. As the song reached its end, the words urged Cassandra's to go forward and start her life with Sandro.

The groom waited patiently at the far end of the court; just in front of a makeshift alter. He stood proud as Cassandra turned slowly. Her angelic radiance seemed to portray two thousand years of beauty. The room broke out in applause as the bride entered and walked toward Sandro, with Oliver holding her arm, tightly. The exquisite triangular necklace that now rested on Cassandra's breast sparkled as if the sapphires and diamonds were powered by a magical source. It was the very artifact that had been perched around the neck of Isis. The gems brilliance blinked in the warm September sun, while they stepped in-and-out of the shadows made by the many columns. Cassandra's hair fell long and dark under a saffron veil. Her gown was white and elegant, resting just below her shoulders and finished with a touch of gold at the end of the train. She stood in tall, gold shoes that pushed her height in order to inch closer to that of her soon-to-be husband. As Oliver backed away, he could no longer hold back his tears. Though Sandro and Cassandra were married earlier before the eyes of God, this time, as they stood in front of their friends and relatives, the moment became breathtaking for all. As they stood hand-in-hand, a certain closeness and finality was felt by those who knew about the tragedy that had separated the lives of Parosius and Veturia so many centuries ago.

A young Roman ring bearer—better known as Cassandra's niece—walked slowly down the isle. She carefully held a silver platter. The young girl handed it to Father Pucci. On the platter was a large bracelet and ring, both made of polished gold. Cassandra and Sandro immediately recognized the artifacts as those of Parosius and Veturia. They looked surprisingly at Professor Stowald who nodded his head and smiled. Sandro slipped the ring on Cassandra's finger while she pushed the bracelet onto Sandro's wrist. For the wedding guests, it was a night they would remember always. For the wedding couple, it only just began.

As the evening wound down and the guests departed, the newlyweds escaped to the oecus room. The room that held the tall statue of Isis was well cleaned, but the floor remained severely cracked from the weight of the debris that had been resting on top of it for nearly two thousand years. A dozen unlit candles were scattered about the room on top of three rounded marble pedestals. A large rug was placed on the floor at its center. In the corner, opposite of Isis, was a Roman style couch set up for the newlyweds. The only light that shown was through a caricature of Diana, the Roman moon goddess, built into the wall. The half-moon above Diana's head was the only part of her that was open to the outside. A bright moon-beam from the cloudless night was glaring through the opening giving the far wall next to Isis a fuzzy moon-shaped projection.

"It was beautiful, wasn't it?" Cassandra asked Sandro.

"The wedding was wonderful. You are the one who is beautiful, Mrs. Ballantonio."

Cassandra smiled devilishly and began to undo Sandro's belt. "Mrs. Ballantonio thinks that the handsome Italian known as, Mr. Ballantonio and I will be spending a lot of time on that couch over there."

Sandro reached down and kissed Cassandra. It was a long, aching kiss, the kind that makes your mind and body float. They needed to make love now and only there clothes would cause a brief and temporary delay.

Sandro and Cassandra scrambled to remove their layers of Roman wedding attire. When Cassandra reached to undo her shoes, she began to tumble. Sandro moved quickly to catch his bride, but in the darkened room he bumped hard into one of the pedestals, as its candles fell to the floor. The room's marble stands were thought to be secured tightly to the floor by the original builders. The excavation workers just left them as they were. This one however, tilted oddly at an angle, but did not tip over.

Cassandra regained her balance and together they looked at the strange pedestal. Seconds later the floor began to rumble. The goddess Isis dropped into the floor. Then as Isis descended, another large statue rose.

When the screeching sound from ancient mechanical design subsided, Sandro and Cassandra lost their romantic intensity and held each other with strained eyes.

"What just happened?"

"I don't know. We need light," Sandro said, lighting the candles.

Dust filled the room. The goddess Isis was now gone. Sandro walked his candle to the statue that had sprung up a few feet from where Isis had been.

"It is Janus, the guardian of exits and entrances."

The Roman god was of two heads facing back-to-back. Each had a beard and appeared identical, save the eyes. One looked up and out in the distance, while the other looked down as if scanning the doorway. Janus' left hand reached out with its palm facing down. The right hand was palm-up and held an image of a key. Except for a chipped nose on one of the faces the marble statue stood the test of time. Sandro and Cassandra began to brush the dirt and dust away from the god. Cassandra saw it first. At the base, just above the written *Ianus* was a key hole.

"You'd better call Oliver…and call the professor as well."

'What is it, Cassandra?"

"It's a key hole, and I'm willing to bet that the key that Mee had around her neck will fit into it."

22

A few days before the big wedding, Oliver was digging deep into the mystery of St. Peter's sword. He studied the path that Veturia may have taken from her villa to her eventual resting place at the beach front. He chronicled any and all historical facts he could find concerning the sword. He persuaded workers to volunteer their time to search along possible areas of interest with metal detectors. He studied the papyri fragments over and over in the hope of finding something that might have been missed. His frustrations were mounting when he received a call from Mee Lee's doctor.

"It's about Mee Lee. You better come to the hospital."

"What is it? Is she getting worse? Is she ...,"

"Quite the contrary, Mr.Taneschio, she's coming out of her coma."

Just days earlier, the doctors at Ospedale Cardinale Ascalesi did not have much hope for her. Oliver drove up the coast, north along the Corso San Giavonni, and arrived at the hospital in a very short time.

Oliver stood next to Mee's twin-sized hospital bed and noticed her face had returned its color to her. Her long red hair was greasy and darker at the roots. A bandage still covered the back of her head where a small plate was placed and her skin stitched up. She opened her eyes and fixed them on the old man to her left.

"How long have you been there?"

"Not long. You look good for someone who nearly left us."

"I feel like I'm in the middle of the mother of all hangovers." The key that once was around her neck now dangled around Oliver's. "I see you haven't found a home for my key."

Oliver looked down at it. "You should have been an archeologist. I've never seen such skill."

"A good thief should be knowledgeable of many things." Mee looked harder at Oliver. At first she thought it was the shadow from the desk lamp, but now she could see his tired, drawn appearance. "How long have you been looking for it?"

"The sword...not nearly long enough."

"Your grandfather and I had something in common. He was a thief. He stole from Italy. He may have had his reasons, but he stole just the same."

Her words didn't hurt Oliver. They clarified something in his mind. He now knew, without any doubt, why Demetri sent him the golden box so many years ago. He was to make it right. "When someone, anyone, makes a monumental mistake, on purpose or not, it can affect much of what happens in life after the fact. Sometimes what is done is done. Other times you are given the chance to correct things." For the first time in weeks Oliver smiled. "Thanks, Mee, you're right. He did something that changed a lot of lives, including yours. Had he not stolen the papyri, our family might have stayed in Italy. Had we stayed here, your brother would be alive today. I can't bring your brother back, but there are some things I *can* do. Get well. I'll see you in a few days."

Oliver left the hospital that day with a new purpose. After the wedding he excused himself from the reception and went back to the hospital to bring Mee some cake. As he approached her bed he was startled to see her police guard sitting in a chair, handcuffed and covered in bandage tape from head to toe. His gun was missing from its holster. Oliver turned around and saw a glimpse of Mee down the hall looking like a typical visitor. As the elevator door closed in front of her she blinked at him and put her finger to her lips in a gesture of quiet. He would help Mee this time, but he wasn't going to make it a habit.

Oliver turned to look at the guard. "I'll send help…eventually," he said whispering the last word. He closed the door behind him and left. When he got into his car he heard his cell phone ring and put it on speaker mode. It was Cassandra.

"Grandpa, can you come to the villa? It's…well…you have to see it."

"Cassandra, it's been a long time since my own wedding night, but I'm pretty sure yours should not include me," he quipped.

"Ordinarily I would agree with you, but it's the statue of Janus. We've found it. Oh, and bring the key."

"I'll be right there."

"This is working out much better than I would have guessed," Mee said from the back seat, startling Oliver.

"You'll be caught again, Mee. I'll drop you anywhere you need to go, but then you're on your own."

Mee pointed the guard's gun at Oliver. "I prefer to go to the Fortunatus Villa please. Isn't it enough that I missed Cassy's wedding, now you want me to miss out on this. I don't think so."

The fifteen-minute drive seemed to take a lifetime. Mee kept looking behind her to see if the authorities were on to them.

"You didn't call the police, why?"

"Why would I call the police? I saw a man in a room watching television," Oliver glanced back. "I'm not looking to pay you back for your brother's death. That was an accident. But, I believe you are a good person. Somewhere inside of you…."

"Forget I asked. You don't owe me a thing. We're good, let's leave it at that."

When they arrived at the villa the dust was not yet settled. The room was now well-lit and the newlyweds stood in front of the large statue. Oliver came into the room first followed by Mee. Professor Stowald was also called and had gotten to the villa just moments before.

Cassandra saw what was happening and said, "Mee, this is getting old. Do you ever walk into a room without a gun?"

Mee let that comment slide and made an attempt to smile through obvious head pain. Oliver examined the statue of Janus and marveled at the two headed god.

"It is here," Sandro said pointing at the key hole.

Oliver removed the key from around his neck and pushed it into the hole. He turned it slowly. A clicking sound was heard and a marble panel below jutted out just a bit. Sandro ran out to his truck and returned with a crow bar. He stuck it into the top edge and leveraged the top. The panel was hinged at the bottom and fell open. Inside was a large chest. Sandro removed the chest and all eyes were then transfixed on its contents. Resting on top of countless necklaces, bracelets, cups, plates, and rings was a sword. The handle alternated in its makeup from fish bone to marble. The top was made into the head of a fish. Just under the handle an oval brass piece marked with the look of fish scales held the blade firmly in place. The blade was eighteen inches in length and nearly two inches wide, coming to a curved point. Both sides of the blade were sharp, as if it was a machete. One side however, had several inches of saw teeth. Etched between the blade and the handle was 'Petros'.

"This is most certainly the sword of Simon-Peter," Oliver said in a shaky voice.

"We must inform the Vatican," Dr. Stowald said.

"Hold on there. No one is doing anything until I say so," Mee said still pointing the pistol. She reached into her pocket and pulled out a small digital camera. She took a picture of the sword and began to leave.

"Where are you going," Oliver asked.

"I just wanted to see it and...I saw it." She looked at Oliver's puzzled expression. "Your right, Oliver... a girl can't live on pictures."

She went back to the chest and took a few choice artifacts. "Once a thief...."

They watched her leave and wondered how far she would get before getting caught.

23

The Vatican was skeptical and cautious in how they proceeded with the sword, but between the papyri fragments, the cup, and the sword itself, little doubt was left. There were several more aging tests and other checks to be completed, but the Vatican was extremely excited about this find. For the time being, however, the sword of St. Peter would be left untouched until proper paperwork could be completed.

On the night before the sword was to be permanently housed in the Vatican, Oliver received a pass from the guards at the entrance of the villa and stood before the relic that his grandfather spent so much of his life looking for. He wondered what Demetri would have done had he found the prized sword. It isn't the type of thing a person puts on his mantle over the fireplace. Perhaps it was the search itself that drove his grandfather to extremes. Oliver made the sign of the cross, then reached down, and for a brief moment, put his right hand around the sword's handle and lifted the relic. He felt a sense of strength and power knowing he was holding the sword of all the stories his grandfather told him as a child. More importantly, he held the holy sword of St. Peter, something that no human had done since August of AD79. As he reached down to place it back into the chest, he heard the light tapping of shoes coming his way. Oliver backed away into the darkness, still holding the sword. He could see an undersized guard walk to the statue of Janus and stand before the chest of artifacts. The guard took a sword from inside his long jacket and quietly laid it on the floor near Oliver's dark seclusion. He then removed his hat revealing long red hair and the fact that the guard was not a man at all.

"I see you've decided that just *seeing* the sword was not enough," Oliver said to Mee.

Mee turned as Oliver stepped out of the shadow. "Perhaps you were having similar thoughts," Mee said seeing the sword in his hand. The sword she placed on the floor looked to be an exact duplicate. "Give it to me, Oliver. I can arrange it so my buyer lets you see it any time you want. You may not be as lucky with the Vatican. Once they have it, you may never see it again."

"I let you escape the police once, Mee. Don't push your luck."

Mee reached to her side and pulled out a gun.

"You wouldn't shoot me. The guards outside would be in here in seconds."

"They think I'm one of them. I'm only shooting someone who is stealing a most valuable artifact. By the time they figure it out I'll be gone."

"You're probably right." Oliver walked over toward Mee and tossed the sword into the chest.

"You're just delaying the inevitable, Oliver," Mee said reaching into the chest for the sword.

As she reached in, Oliver pushed on the pedestal as hard as he could. The statue of Janus descended with Mee clinging to it. Mee looked at the sword Oliver threw to her and turned to give Oliver an odd wink before disappearing. Within seconds a floor board covered the statue, entombing Mee.

The police guards ran inside to see what was happening.

"You'll find the American thief you've been looking for under the floor. She was after the sword. She'll have a gun with her," Oliver said as he walked away. The Vatican guards watched him for a while, and then turned their attention to Mee Lee.

Oliver left the villa and walked along the coast, his overcoat protecting him from a cool, brisk wind. The more he walked, the better he felt about how his life played out. He thought about his grandfather, the sword, and its legacy. Given a chance, perhaps the sword would someday save another life and the stories of his grandfather Demetri could go on.

For a while, the Vatican believed it had their most coveted possession. But subsequent testing found that although the sword itself dated back to the correct time, there were inconsistencies with the sword handle. They decided not to proclaim it as the real thing.

Years later, Oliver sat in his easy chair in front of the fireplace that burned brightly in his country home. Two of his great-grandchildren, from Sandro and Cassandra, huddled in the chair with him. There, as with every Sunday, he told them a story about an ancient sword. Above the fireplace a sword rests, securely fastened to the wall.

AUTHOR'S NOTE

Stress between two huge blocks of the earth's crust, or plates, have been colliding for centuries. With one plate carrying Africa, and the other Eurasia, the clash forced the edge of the Mediterranean Sea down into the depths of the earth. This action created Vesuvius and many more volcanoes.

Vesuvius remains high above all that rests below. Its peaceful and lush green carpet masking what lies deep inside. An occasional puff of smoke and steam spews out to remind those who dare to forget its propensity for disaster.

Over its history Vesuvius stood by, watching and waiting. It remained relatively quiet until AD 202 when it erupted for a week. After a major eruption in AD 533, the next occurrence came in 1631. Nearly as violent as the eruption of AD 79, as many as 18,000 people may have fallen under seven streams of lava. The last eruption was in 1944.

It looms over men and women who live and love, cheat death or get cheated by it, play, dance, work, vacation, and toil in an ever-changing world. Around thirty thousand people lived in its vicinity in AD 79. Now over three million could be seriously affected by the next eruption. Ercolano rests above Herculaneum and boasts fifty-six thousand inhabitants. The population of the modern town of Pompei is now at about twenty-seven thousand.

In AD 79, Vesuvius spewed debris for eighteen hours and dropped ten billion tons of ash, pumice, and rock. Could it happen again?

I set out to tell a story about the lives of Romans during the time of disaster. I ended up with a deep desire to humanize a Roman couple and have their lives make a profound connection to those that live in the present.

My two young Romans lived in a world where blood sports were the entertainment of the day. Slaves of all races and color were ridiculed, tortured and abused like animals. Most women were treated only as tools to bear children, and many died early in their lives performing that task.

To some degree parts of our world still subscribe to the ways the Romans lived—both bad and good. Many of their human traits and morals remain. Despite the family structure that held the father of the house as the commander and chief of all life decisions, some people did find love. They ate, drank, laughed, prayed, and argued much as we do now. Just as Parosius and Veturia found each other and had at least a measure of happiness together, so, too, Cassandra and Sandro traveled down life's path.

Herculaneum is still largely unexcavated. The relics, treasures, and historical value yet to be discovered, leaves much to the imagination. Are the pearl of Cleopatra and the sword of St. Peter waiting to be unearthed—maybe? Will future archaeologists be allowed to further reveal what Vesuvius hid? It sure would be something, wouldn't it?

I thank the authors of the many books and internet sites I've researched in order to put myself into a time in history that is still exciting and intriguing to many.

Vesuvius will do what it will do, just as we humans will. Despite man's pertinacity to consider himself the emperor of this planet, his technical abilities and preparedness can do little in preventing another volcanic disaster. Perhaps someday technology will triumph, but not today. The people under the great mountain know that their homes are only a temporary abode. Many, who do not dwell there, wonder how one can live with the possibility of devastation. I, on the other hand, salute those that live not with the certainty of doom, but by taking each day as a gift and go on without regret!

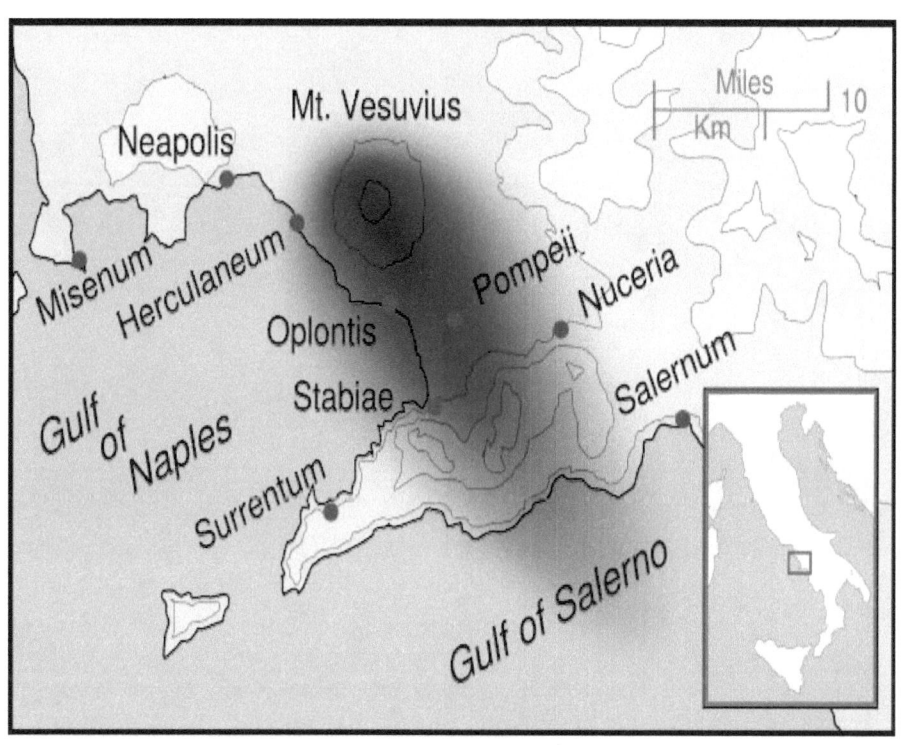

This map depicts where Vesuvius blanketed the area with debris in AD 79.